Marilyn Lee Unleashed Presents

D1706466

# Shana Mine

# Marilyn Lee

F
Lee
$15⁰⁰

1/14

0201704

ISBN-13: 978-1475239690
ISBN-10: 1475239696

Shana Mine

# Chapter One

"I must be hearing things." I stared at the woman seated in one of the two chairs opposite my desk in silence for several moments. Best friends since kindergarten, we were so close that in every way that mattered, we were sisters of the heart and soul, if not by blood. I'd even named my daughter after her.

We generally did anything for each other but what she wanted now was too much — especially after all the intimate stories I'd heard. I shook my head. "Come again. You want me to do what?"

"Oh come on, Shana. Don't look at me as if I've lost my mind."

"Either you've lost yours or you think I've lost mine," I said, trying to sound and look resolute.

As usual, Jasmin quickly came up with a reason why she shouldn't take no for an answer. "A change of scenery will do you good."

Since ending a three-year relationship six months earlier, I'd been struggling to overcome loneliness and boredom so I could get my life back on an even keel. After a lot of heartache and too many sleepless nights, I finally felt ready to share my life and bed with a man again.

Although I didn't have any particular prospects in sight, I didn't want to put my plans on hold to do her another favor. "I don't need a change so badly that I'm prepared to fly across the country to do your dirty work," I said.

"If you do this, I promise I'll never ask you to do anything ever again."

Ever since I could remember, Jasmin had been asking and expecting me to do favors for her. Rarely able to say no to her, I generally did them. Of course, the favor thing worked both ways. I'd talked her into doing some things for me she didn't want to do once or twice. Still, I think we'd both agree that she tended to ask for more favors than I did. "Never is a long time and I don't recall you going for more than a few weeks without needing a favor," I reminded her.

She grimaced and then nodded. "Okay. You're right, but honestly, Shana, Taylor's a great guy and he deserves to hear the truth in person."

I shrugged. Although I'd never let on, her sensual tales of the man she was about to dump had sent me reaching for my BOB on more than one night since my break up from Tremain Younger, the sexy stud I'd almost imagined myself in love with. His dumping me for another woman had soon cured me of that delusion.

A lonely woman could only hear so many stories of a handsome, sexy Native American hunk who loved his women dark-skinned and full-figured before she found herself engaging in forbidden activities—namely fantasizing about spending a night in the arms of her best friend's man.

Feeling my cheeks burn at my thoughts, I shrugged again and tried to appear disinterested. "So tell him." I glanced at my watch to give her a reminder that I had a nine to five job I needed to get back to instead of discussing her love life.

"Are you listening, Shana?"

I nodded, giving her my full attention. As usual, both her hair and make-up were as flawless as was the beautifully made pantsuit that flattered her full-figured body. It was attractive, confident women like Jasmin who helped put plus-size women on the cover of fashion magazines and put men on notice that we could stir their passions too, I thought with sisterly pride.

Although thirty-nine, Jasmin looked ten years younger, which probably accounted for her having caught and held Taylor Raymond's attention–even though he was nine years her junior.

"Shana?"

I sighed inwardly, mentally preparing myself to remain firm. I owned a cleaning company that was finally successful enough to allow me to devote most of my energies to doing what I'd always wanted to do — write an erotic romance with a hero who couldn't keep his big, hot hands off the sexy, confident plus-size heroine.

I'd hired and trained an office manager who had taken over the day–to–day management of the business, allowing me more time to write. "My novel is going really well. I'm not going to lose my momentum by stopping to fly to the East Coast to deliver your Dear John letter." I paused and bit my lip at the exaggeration. While the storyline was coming along well, writing the love scenes was heavy going.

Of course, Jasmin knew that but like the best friend she was she didn't use it against me in an effort to strengthen her case. "You have a laptop and that tablet I bought you for your birthday that you can take with you," she pointed out sweetly.

"Never mind that," I retorted. "Anyway, if this Taylor Raymond is so wonderful, why are you ending your relationship with him in favor of going off with your rich photographer boyfriend?"

"First girl, you know I don't do boys. Both Taylor and Howard are men with all caps, but Howard can open some very important doors for me. At my age, I'm very fortunate to still be able to land assignments. After the European layouts, I'll be in a better position to decide if it's time to say goodbye to modeling and dust off my MBA and put it to work full-time."

"Jasmin —"

"I can't pass up this opportunity, Shana. But in order to take full advantage of what might be my last opportunity, I have to leave tomorrow and be free to travel as needed. That doesn't give me much time to fly to the East Coast to return his bracelet and explain that right now is not a good time for me to start a serious relationship."

"Well, he'll just have to wait to hear the news when you have time," I said.

"He deserves better than that, Shana." She sighed. "We haven't slept together for over four months and I've hinted that I don't have time for more."

"Then why take that bracelet which must have cost close to a grand?"

"Because it's beautiful and at the time he gave it to me, I wanted more than I now have time for," she said, sounding defensive.

"Why take an expensive present before you were ready for an exclusive relationship with him?"

She shook her head. "Asking the question a different way won't change the answer. Look, wait until you meet him. He's sexy as hell, great in bed, and he can be very persuasive. Why else would I have gone out with him more than a few times? You know he's not my type."

I'd never known Jasmin to date a non-black male more than a few times. On the one hand, the fact that she'd engaged in a long distance relationship with this Taylor Raymond for nearly a year said a lot about the effect he must have had on her. On the other hand, she'd gone out of her way to make sure he and I never met. I had to think that said something about her lack of interest in a serious relationship with him.

"I hear what you're saying, Jas, but I'm not interested in making this my problem."

She stared at me, her gaze narrowed. "Girl, get a grip. Since when are there *my problems* and *your problems* instead of *our problems*?"

"Since never, " I admitted. "but what were you thinking Jas? What did you think you'd have in common with a handyman?"

"He's not just a handyman," she said. "Like you, he owns his own company. Yes, he still has to get those big, hot hands of his dirty sometimes, but it's his company. Just as you've made a success of your company, so will he." She arched a brow and gave me a long look. "Actually, you own a cleaning company and he owns a handyman one. The two of you should get on like a house on fire."

"Nice try, but I can't get away right now."

"Shana, you have to do this for me. He's been…dumped before."

*And you know what that's like.* Of course, she didn't actually say the words aloud but we both felt the words hanging between us.

She removed the beautiful tennis bracelet from her wrist with obvious reluctance and handed it to me. "Please, you have to go and let him down, Shana. You have such a pleasing way that this is bound to sting less coming from you."

Maybe that was why I'd had trouble landing and keeping a man since my divorce. If so, clearly it was time to stop being so soothing and concentrate on turning myself into a sexy siren. Call me old-fashioned but I wanted to know my man loved me enough to marry me.

"Shana?"

Oh hell. I'd never been able to deny Jasmin anything for very long. So even though the thought of delivering a Dear John letter to a man I'd never met but couldn't stop fantasizing about held little appeal, I sighed and finally agreed. "I'll go—under duress and girl are you going to owe me big time."

Jasmin sighed in relief and reached across the desk to grip my hand. "Thanks, Shana. I know this is a bit of a pain, but once you meet Taylor, I think you'll understand why it was so difficult to say no to him in person."

I cast my gaze ceiling–ward. "If you've seen one man you've seen them all," I said.

"Tell me that after you've met him. He's the complete package: tall, handsome, and sexy as hell. Better still, he has a big, hard pussy-pleasing cock," she said, licking her lips.

I stared at her and then laughed. "Girl, you are too damn old to be so easily sidetracked by a man just because he's well-hung."

"Hey, get a grip, Shana. A straight woman is never too old to get excited by a big cock. Besides, there's well-hung and then there's Taylor Raymond's delicious cock," she said, grinning. "I swear, if he were a few years older and black, I'd have branded his ass and his cock as my exclusive property the moment I felt that big dick of his sliding so deep in me."

"Oh stop or you'll make me jump his bones the moment we meet," I said, still laughing but only half–jokingly.

She shrugged. "If you get a chance, go for it, girl," she said.

"Oh please, Jas. Like I'm going to hop into bed with a male only nine years older than my son."

"We're talking about a romp in bed, not a lifetime commitment. If you get the chance to bed him, you'd better take it or trust me, you'll always regret it."

"Will you stop already?"

"Listen, girl. We've both had relationships with well-hung men. There are quite a few of them around. Unfortunately, not all of them know how to use their best asset effectively. He does. We're talking cockasaurus-rex coupled with a level of skill that's off the charts, girl. We're talking Pointer Sisters' Slow Hand here. The man is not selfish when it comes to pleasing a woman."

"Jas!" Even as I protested, I couldn't dismiss a mental picture of a handsome, naked Native American male with a huge, hard shaft he knew how to use. After so many months of celibacy, such thoughts left me longing for a hard, raunchy fuck.

"No. Believe me, Shana, spend one night with him and all bets about not dating younger men will be off—just as all bets about not dating non-black men more than once were off for me."

I held up a hand. "Enough talk of sex. I don't have time to take a cold shower. I'll go to Philadelphia, but you're going to owe me big time."

She nodded. "Deal, now I'll get out of your hair." She rose, kissed my cheek, and left quickly—probably afraid I'd come to my senses and change my mind.

Alone in my office, I got up and went into the attached bathroom.

Standing in front of the full-length mirror on my wall, I studied myself.

I was tall and thick. Hell, maybe full-figured. I had big legs and what my ex had called a bootylicious butt. The features I was most proud of were my large, natural breasts and the long, dark hair that ended well past my shoulders—all mine. I had dark, smooth skin and a face most men found attractive.

Back in my office, I sat with my head against the back of the chair with my eyes closed. *You are a piece of work. One of these days you're going to have to learn to say no to Jas and mean it.* Recalling the last minutes of our conversation, my panties flooded. *Oh God, to feel a big, hard cock inside me again would rock my world. But you are not going to hop into bed with a man who's already bedded your best friend. So get a damned grip, Shana.*

I opened my eyes and forced my thoughts back to work. Three hours later, as I was about to leave the office for the day, Jasmin called.

"I've made all the arrangements for your trip to Philadelphia," she said. "All expenses are paid for a week. Do you need money for food now or can you wait until I return?"

"I'm going to give him the bad news and then head back to the airport. I only need one night at the hotel."

"You can't fly across the country and only stay a few hours. I booked you in for a week. Trust me, once you meet him, you'll be glad you're not stuck with just an over– nighter.

"If I know you, you're not going to hop into bed with him the first night. So you'll need more than one night."

"Will you give it a rest?" I snapped.

"Excuse me for breathing," she said.

I rolled my eyes. "One day or six, I can pay for my own meals."

"Are you sure? You're only going as a favor to me."

"I know that but I can pay for my own meals."

"Okay. Well…do me proud and let him down gently. Then fuck me right out of his mind during the week."

*Wouldn't I love to do just that?* I outlined my top lip with my tongue. "I have no interest in staying more than one night."

"Use the time to sightsee. The Liberty Bell and the Constitution Center are within walking distance of your hotel. The Reading Terminal Market has to be seen to be believed. It's historic and filled with all kinds of restaurants. Taylor and I enjoyed going on horse-driven carriage rides too. We visited the Betty Rose and the Poe House. There's a lot of history you'll enjoy exploring with or without."

"With or without what?"

"Taylor. He's a bit of a workaholic but with the right incentive, maybe you can convince him to take some time off."

"Did you?"

"No," she admitted. "All our sightseeing took place after work or on the weekends."

"I doubt he'll want to spend any quality time with me after I've delivered the bad news."

"Maybe not but if he wants to bed you, go for it. Just do me a favor and make sure you don't fall for him."

"Why not?"

"Because I might decide I want him back and I don't want any problems between us if that happens. Fuck him but do not fall for him because I might want him back."

I frowned. Sometimes Jasmin had a habit of treating her lovers like possessions rather than equal partners. "There's not much chance of that happening," I assured her. "Anyway, have a great shoot and a wonderful time, Jas."

"You too, Shana. I'll see you when I return."

"I'll be here, girl," I said and hung up.

I went home to have dinner, pack, and call my son and daughter to tell them I'd be heading out of town for a while. My twenty-year-old twins, Jassy and Jimmy, would start their senior year of college in the fall.

Jassy urged me to have a wild time. "Let your hair down, Mom and live a little."

I knew what she meant by live a little. Like Jasmin, she thought I was taking too long to get over Tremain. "We'll see," I said. "I'll call you when I get back. Now I need to call your brother. Love you."

"I love you too, Mom," she said.

Smiling, I dialed her brother's number.

Jimmy listened in silence before he spoke. "Despite the advice I know Jassy gave you, please be careful, Mom. There's no rush to start a new relationship. You can take your time and get it right."

Oh but I was more than ready to take another lover. "Don't worry about me, sweetie."

"I do worry," he said. "It's part of my job."

Since my divorce, ten years earlier, despite my assurances, Jimmy had felt he had to look after me. "Don't worry," I said again.

"Promise me you'll call me if you need anything."

Hell would freeze over before I burdened either of my kids with my problems. "Of course, sweetie. I'll see you soon."

"Call or text me to let me know you arrived safely."

"I will. Love you, sweetie."

"Love you, Mom."

Later that night I fell asleep and had a series of erotic dreams where a faceless man with a big shaft cocked me all night long until I nearly screamed the place down. My heart thumped and my panties were wet when I woke because I knew the faceless man of my dreams had been Taylor Raymond.

*Get a grip, girl. You cannot start thinking with your pussy.*

Groaning with frustration, I rolled onto my stomach and drifted to sleep again—and dreamed of Taylor Raymond again.

A day later, I arrived in Philadelphia after a six-hour flight from San Francisco. At the last moment, I'd decided to take Jasmin's advice and packed enough clothes for a week's vacation. After I saw Taylor Raymond in the morning, I'd get down to some serious sightseeing. And just maybe I might even let my hair down enough to get my freak on in a one-night stand. Or two. Hell, maybe three. *But not with Taylor Raymond, girl. Not with him. That would create too many problems.*

Hoping I'd wrestled my emotions and fantasies under sufficient control that Taylor Raymond would not know I'd been spending far too much time daydreaming about him; I collected my bags and boarded the airport shuttle to my Center City hotel.

I was pleasantly surprised to find that Jas had booked me a small suite. Placing my bags near the closet, I sat down to send a quick email to Jimmy and Jassy to let them know I'd arrived safely and would see them in a week.

Then I went down to the hotel restaurant. While having a salad and a beer, I noticed a lone handsome man with dark skin and eyes seated at a table facing mine giving me a fair amount of attention.

Lonely and ready for a little male companionship, I would have been receptive if he approached me. He didn't but I left the restaurant confident that there was always tomorrow. Hopefully, his stay would extend long enough for us to meet before I went home. And maybe the next time we met, I'd make a move if he didn't.

Back in my suite, I undressed and took a long soak. Lying in the warm, soothing water, I closed my eyes and imagined myself wrapped in the arms of Mr. Dark, handsome and sexy. I allowed my imagination to weave a super sensual dream around the man from the restaurant before the cooling water spurred me to get out of the bath and go to bed.

Relaxed by the soak, I fell asleep almost immediately but woke in the middle of the night longing to feel a big, hard body pressed against mine. Despite my efforts to corral my thoughts, I couldn't stop thinking about Taylor Raymond. His was the body I wanted to feel crushing mine to the bed. I wanted to explore the mystique of the Native American lover with him.

*If you're going to develop a thing for a Native male, it can't be Jasmin's.* Despite her encouraging me to sleep with him, neither of us had ever crossed that line. We were too damned close to risk our relationship over a man. I sighed and rolled onto my side and tried to clear my thoughts of hot sex with Taylor Raymond until I finally fell asleep again.

# Chapter Two

The next morning, just before nine, I waited in the corridor outside Taylor Raymond's office. Jasmin said he usually spent a few hours there on Saturday mornings catching up on paperwork.

When I heard the elevator door open, I turned to see a tall, well-built man coming down the hallway towards me. I'm five-nine and love to display my legs whenever I can by wearing heels. I didn't get to do that often since even three-inch heels would make me taller than a man of average height.

The man heading towards me had to be at least six feet and two inches tall of pure, sexy hunk. His sleek, dark hair was pulled back from his handsome face. His dark eyes seemed to reach out to pull me into their depths. And he stalked rather than walked down the hall with all the confidence of a man certain of his appeal to the opposite sex. But I knew he'd look just as charismatic on a big horse with his hair hanging past his magnificent shoulders.

Taylor Raymond. Oh Lord. Jasmin must have taken complete leave of every one of her senses. What woman worth the name would ever consider walking away from him? Thoughts of hot, raw sex filled my head and made it difficult not to allow my gaze to fall below his waist.

He wore jeans and a pullover that highlighted his long legs and his very well defined upper body. Damn. I wanted to strip naked and offer myself as his sex slave — forever.

*Stop it! There will be no gawking, girl. None. Give him the bad news and take your horny behind back to the hotel and pray you run into Mr. Tall, Dark, and Handsome from the restaurant.*

Taking a deep breath, I pasted a smile on my face and he stopped in front of me. "Taylor Raymond?"

He nodded, his dark eyes making a swift inspection of my body before locking his gaze on mine.

I extended my hand.

He inhaled slowly. "And you're Shana Morgan."

Surprised, I nodded, allowing my hand to drop to my side. How the hell did he know who I was? If Jas had called him and told him I was coming, why ask me to come at all? "Ah…yes. I am."

"Jasmin's best friend."

"That's me." I extended my hand again.

He took it and held it clasped between both of his while he stared at me.

A shiver of desire shot through me at the contact and I could neither muster the will to remove my hand from his or to look away from his dark, seductive gaze.

"Why are you here instead of her?"

"She regrets that she couldn't come so she asked me to."

"I kind of figured she wasn't coming when she didn't show up three days ago and failed to take my calls."

Oh hell. She hadn't said a damned thing about ignoring his calls. "I came in her place."

"So I see." He arched a brow. "Judging by the solemn look on your lovely face, you're here as the bearer of what's supposed to be bad news."

The compliment, spoken in his deep, honeyed voice thrilled me. While I knew most men found me attractive, not many men considered me lovely—at least not when compared to Jasmin who would probably be as stunning at eighty as she was now.

Supposed to be bad news? I frowned—unsure what to make of that remark.

He took a key out of his pocket. "You'd better come into the office. My secretary doesn't work on Saturdays so we can talk."

Talking wasn't at the top of my list of things I'd like to do with him, but I smiled and nodded.

He ushered me into his office and pointed towards a loveseat along one wall before walking to a small refrigerator in one corner. "Would you like some juice or do you want me to make coffee?" he asked, standing in front of the open door.

"Thanks, but I'm fine."

He closed the door of the refrigerator and crossed the room to the loveseat. Instead of sitting beside me, which I both wanted and feared, he stood over me in silence.

I took a deep breath before I took the jeweler's box holding the tennis bracelet out of my shoulder bag and held it out to him.

He made no effort to speak or to take it.

Great. He was going to make this difficult. "I'm sorry but I don't know of an easy way to say this except to come right out with it."

"Go right ahead then."

"Jasmin is out of the country doing a photo shoot. Although she really likes you, now is just not the time for a serious relationship. So she asked me to bring this back to you and explain."

"Explain that she was more than a little drunk when she accepted it?" He sat beside me but made no effort to take the box. "What happened? Did she sober up and decide my job isn't high-powered enough for her?"

"Oh no!" I placed a hand on his arm. "Jasmin isn't like that."

He gave me a cool stare. "Isn't she?"

"No! She's not. I told you her reason for not being here."

"If that were her only reason, why is she returning the bracelet? Why didn't she at least give me the consideration of calling herself? Why send you to kick my ass to the curb?"

Although he looked and sounded annoyed, I could detect no evidence that his heart was broken. "That's not why I came. She asked and I agreed to come because we both wanted to make this as easy for you as possible."

"Guess what? Having you here does absolutely nothing to soothe what you both probably consider my battered emotions."

Well damn. Wasn't he the charming one? "Look, I know this isn't easy for you."

"But?"

But it was almost impossible to think straight with him sitting so close. "But as you must know, you're handsome and…well put…together. You're not going to have any problems finding another woman…eager to help you get over her."

He turned his head to look at me.

I stared back, wondering what he'd look like with his long, dark brown hair spilling over those broad shoulders. Imagining them bare and accessible to touch and caress, aroused me. I looked at his mouth and longed to lean forward and kiss him until he couldn't breathe.

Feeling my cheeks heat up, I pushed the jeweler's box in his hands and quickly rose. "I'm so sorry I wasn't able to make this easier for you."

He inhaled softly and lowered his lashes. "Oh hell." He looked down.

I'd done as Jasmin had asked me to do. So I was perfectly justified in just walking out and leaving him to recover in private. Curling my right hand into a fist to keep from caressing his hair, I walked across the carpet.

At the door, I turned for one last look and found him staring at me with an inscrutable look in his eyes. What was he thinking? What was he feeling? *Why the hell should you care? Leave before you do something you can't undo.* There was something about him I couldn't resist. Something that made it impossible to leave.

"Don't go," he said.

"I have to."

"No. You don't." He extended a hand.

I walked to the loveseat and knelt at his side. When I placed my hand on his hard thigh, I intended to offer him comfort. But a jolt of passion shot through me at the contact. I knew he felt it too, because his head jerked up and he stared at me.

Meeting a look in his eyes that blazed with desire, I bit my lip. *What are you doing?* "I have to go."

"You say that as if you think I'm actually going to let you go."

"What?"

He caressed my cheek, brushing his fingers against my lips.

I couldn't stop myself from turning my face into his palm and wishing I was kissing his mouth.

He reached for my hand. "I know you've done what she wanted you to and you want to leave."

I'd never wanted to stay anywhere more.

He squeezed my hand gently. "I know this is unpleasant for you, but if you really want to make this easier for me, please stay."

If I did, God only knew what would happen. I shook my head. "I really have to go."

He slipped off the loveseat and onto his knees in front of me.

*Oh no. Don't.*

His big, warm hands cupped my face. "I need you to stay with me now. Just for a little while. Please."

*You can't – not the way you're feeling.* "Why?"

He stroked his hands down from my cheeks to my neck. "Because I don't want to be alone."

I met his gaze again, saw his desire, and felt my own welling. I totally wanted to stay but if Jasmin decided to reclaim him after I'd slept with him, our relationship might suffer.

He bent his head.

Although I longed to feel his mouth on mine, I shook my head and quickly rose, my heart pounding. "I have to go." *Before I surrender to you.* I rushed towards the door.

He followed me and placed his palm against the closed door. "Where are you staying?" He asked the question with his lips close to my ear.

I leaned my forehead against the door, closing my eyes. *If you tell him that, you might as well stay because you know what's going to happen.*

"Where are you staying, Shana?"

Moistening my lips, I murmured the name of my hotel.

He inhaled softly and pressed his warm lips against the side of my neck.

I shivered, clenching my hands into fists. Oh lord. To feel those firm lips all over my naked body. *Stop, Shana. Stop this now.* "Don't."

"Why not?"

For a moment I couldn't think of a single valid response. "She's my oldest and dearest friend. That's why not," I finally said.

"I'm a quick study. She didn't show up when she promised and she won't answer my calls. Her clear message to me? It's over between us, dumbass."

"Is it?"

"She doesn't want me and even before meeting you, the feeling was mutual." He brushed his lips against my ear. "That's why."

"Why not is because I don't want you either," I said.

"Don't you?"

"No," I lied. "I don't."

He took my arm and turned me around to face him. "Open your eyes and look at me when you utter that lie."

*Great. He knew I was lying.* "Why would I do that?"

"So you can see the desire I feel is for you and not her."

How had I allowed this situation to spiral so close to the brink of disaster so quickly?

"Open your eyes."

I lifted my chin and looked at him. Seeing my reflected desire in his gaze, I was nearly lost. I'd never wanted mindless sex more, but I needed a night's rest and a clear head before I made the decision to go where Jasmin and I had never gone — have sex with a man the other had already slept with.

I pushed against his shoulders. "I'm sorry. I have to go."

To my surprise, he stepped back, allowing his hands to fall to his sides.

I stared at him, almost lost in his sexual allure. Lord he was so big…so attractive…so sexy…so irresistible. My gaze slid down his body and locked on his crotch. The outline of his cock was clear along one leg. And it was a sizable outline. Oh God. To feel that sliding inside me.

I bit my lip and dragged my gaze up to lock with his. "I have to go," I whispered.

"Why when we both want you to stay?"

"I'm going."

He shrugged. "Fine. When you turn the knob, the door behind you opens."

I moistened my lips and turned to open the door. He made no move to stop me and I reluctantly walked out of his office and into the corridor. Suppressing the urge to look over my shoulder, I pushed the elevator call button and stepped inside when the doors opened.

Once inside the elevator, I shuddered and briefly closed my eyes. *Oh lord girl. You have to get a grip.*

I spent the entire trip back to the hotel reliving every second with him. I'd never had such a strong physical attraction to any man — including my ex-husband. That was no reason to rashly do what I'd never be able to undo. Back in my suite, I changed into jeans and a long-sleeved blouse. I put on a pair of running shoes and sat on the loveseat with my phone in my hand. After several minutes of staring at it, I called Jasmin.

"Hey girl, what the hell is going on?" she demanded.

"What do you mean?" I asked warily.

"Taylor just called and read me the riot act."

"He did?"

"He told me he was sick of my shit and that he had no more interest in me than I had in him. Then he told me to fuck off and hung up on me. What happened between you two?"

"What makes you think anything happen?"

"The last time I saw him, there was still some heat between us, and he wanted me to come back to Philly. He meets you and the next thing I know he's telling me to fuck off. That's what makes me think something happened between you two."

The obvious disbelief in her voice would have pissed me off if I didn't feel so guilty. "He expressed some interest but —"

"But you weren't interested?"

I closed my eyes. "I'm horny and lonely and damn girl, he's a hunk."

"So?"

"You've already slept with him."

"That happened nearly five months ago," she said with obvious reluctance.

"You still have some warm feelings for him."

"Actually, I don't know if the feelings are for him or that big cock of his."

"Talk like that isn't helping, Jasmin!"

She sighed. "You know what? You've raised two great kids and kind of put your life on hold while you did. I suppose you're allowed to do what feels good once in awhile."

"So you're back to it's okay to sleep with him? I wish you'd make up your mind!"

"Look, you want to sleep with him? Fine. Do it."

"I won't be able to unsleep with him if you decide you want him after all." The silence that greeted my words unnerved me. "Jas?"

"Yeah. I know," she finally said.

"And? You'd be okay with that?"

"I don't know," she admitted. "But I do know you deserve to unwind and clearly he's pissed off enough with me to want to unwind with you. Go for it. If I decide I want him back later…"

"What?"

"We can arm wrestle for him."

"Jas—"

"Look, I don't know how I'm going to feel or want when I return home. So do what feels right and we'll worry about the consequences later."

"You were angry just a few seconds ago, Jas."

"I was just…surprised that he wanted to jump your bones so quickly, but I'm back on track now. Go get laid, girl. Just try to do me a favor."

"What?"

"Don't fall in love with him—just in case I do want him back."

"What I'm feeling starts with an l but it ain't love, girl," I assured her.

"Lust is natural and nothing to be ashamed of. Go for it. Sleep with him if you want. Lord knows he clearly wants to sleep with you. We've been through so much together that if we find we both want him, we'll work it out."

"How? By sharing him?"

"I don't know how. I just know we will."

"Are you in love with him, Jasmin?"

"No. I'm not and he sure as hell isn't in love with me. Okay?"

It wasn't but there didn't seem to be much point in continuing the discussion. I knew if I saw him again, we'd end up in bed. And what did that say about the strength of my commitment to our long friendship? "I can't lose you as a friend."

"That won't ever happen," she promised. "Even if you killed a few people, I'd still be in your corner—as long as those people didn't include my babies."

My kids loved Jasmin but hated the way she called them her babies—even though they were nearly twenty-one. I sighed. "I might have to hold you to that promise. I'll see you when you get home."

After we ended the call, I felt restless and uncertain what I should do. My desire to hop into bed with Taylor Raymond hadn't lessened a single iota. Still, as much as I wanted him, I kept telling myself I didn't want him enough to strain my relationship with Jasmin.

The wisest course would be to head home and remove myself from all possible temptation. But first I'd spend the next few days exploring the city.

Strapping on a fanny pack, I went down to the lobby, picked up a few sightseeing brochures and went on a walking tour to explore the area around the hotel. I returned to the hotel just after five p. m. My plans for the evening included a quick soak and then dinner at the hotel restaurant.

Those tentative plans vanished when Taylor Raymond rose from one of the lobby chairs as I entered the hotel.

He wore a dark suit with a white shirt and a silk tie. His long, dark hair rested over his broad shoulders. He looked sexy and determined. As our gazes locked, a slow, warm smile spread across his handsome face.

I came to an abrupt halt. My heart pounded. My thong flooded. And I was so lost in him.

He kept walking. When he reached me, he engulfed my hand in his. Then he bent to brush his lips against my cheek. "Shana."

I couldn't remember any potential lover whispering my name with such need and warmth.

He lifted his head. "I came prepared to convince you to have dinner with me," he said.

I disengaged my hand from his and stepped away from him. "Thanks but I already have plans for tonight."

"So do I and they all revolve around you." He reclaimed my hand and brushed his lips against it.

"You slept with my best friend."

"I've slept with a lot of women," he said bluntly.

Annoyed, I jerked my hand away. "That remark doesn't help your case."

"It's not reasonable to hold things that happened before we met against me, Shana."

How could I argue with that logic? "Who you've slept with is no concern of mine." I continued towards the elevator.

He followed me. "I'll wait down here while you do whatever you need to."

I shook my head.

"Please don't give me a complex by dumping me."

I pushed the call button before looking up at him. "In order for me to dump you, there'd have to be something between us and there's not."

"Don't bust my ass," he said. "And let's not play games."

"Who's playing games?"

"You are. We both knew there was something between us the moment we met."

True dat.

"So why waste time denying the obvious?"

He certainly didn't lack confidence. The elevator doors opened. I stepped in without responding.

He reached out a hand to keep the doors from closing. "I'll be waiting, Shana. Don't stand me up."

"If I do?"

"It won't do you any good. I always get what I want. And I want you."

I stared at him. "You do?"

"Hell to the yes." He smiled and stepped back, allowing the doors to slide close.

In my hotel suite, I sank down onto the loveseat. Closing my eyes, I took several slow deep breaths. *You cannot go out with him. You can't.*

The phone rang.

Startled, I sat up and picked up the phone. "Hello?"

"Why aren't you in the shower instead of answering the phone?"

Persistent and attractive. And so sexy I just had to have him.

"Shana?"

My decision made, I rose slowly. "Give me an hour."

"Make it forty minutes and we have a deal."

"Forty minutes," I promised. Smiling, I put the phone down and rushed to the bathroom to take a quick shower.

Fifty minutes later, he met me in the lobby with a beautiful bouquet and a warm smile that made me imagine all manner of things—none of them utterable in polite company. "You look exquisite," he said.

"So do you." Good enough to spend all night fucking.

He gave me the flowers and offered me his arm.

I hesitated. Once I left with him, there would be no going back.

"It was over between Jasmin and me months ago. That's why she wouldn't take my calls and why I didn't pursue her or do anything to try to change her mind. It's just starting between you and me." He offered me his arm again.

Mentally clinging to Jasmin's promise that our friendship could withstand my sleeping with him, I slipped my arm through his.

Smiling, he gently squeezed it against his body.

I looked up into his dark eyes and felt like a teenage girl crushing the entire night. Every time I met his gaze, I struggled not to lose myself in sexy fantasies. We had dinner on the patio of a historic restaurant overlooking the river. I was only conscious of him seated across from me alternatively staring and smiling with an intimacy that kept me aroused and eager for the night to end—with us in bed.

After the meal, we danced slow and close together. But he surprised me by making no attempt to grind against me or fondle me. He kept his hands above my waist and his lips to himself—which annoyed the hell out of me. Who wanted a big, handsome hunk to behave like a gentleman while dancing under the stars?

"I'm in the mood for a drive. Are you interested?" he asked as he led me back to our table after our last dance.

I was a little old to park and cuddle, but what the hell. I had no doubt it would be thrilling with him. "Yes," I said.

After a drive, he parked in a secluded spot in a large park and then the damned man wanted to talk. Not undress or fondle me and fuck me senseless but talk!

"Tell me about yourself," he said, staring ahead into the darkness surrounding us.

I took a slow, calming breath, and told him about myself — including the fact that I had two twenty-year old kids.

"I understand they're both destined for great things," he said, turning his head to smile at me.

"I'm sure they are, but how do you know that?"

He shrugged. "Jasmin told me."

"She did?"

He nodded. "She thinks you and your kids are the best thing since sliced bread. That's how I recognized you yesterday morning."

"She described me?"

"She did better than that. She showed me your picture — which totally enchanted me."

I blinked at him. "My picture enchanted you after you'd met and slept with her?"

"You ask that as if you expect to be less attractive to men than she is."

"Hello. She's a model. I'm not."

"She's a beautiful woman," he admitted. "But she's...she's..."

"She's my best friend," I reminded him. He needed to know that I had no interest in hearing anything bad about her.

"She's not as...natural as you are," he finished. "A woman doesn't need to wear false eyelashes, excessive make-up, or overly suggestive clothes to catch and hold my attention. Hell, she doesn't even have to be pretty." He paused and gave me a long look. "The fact that you're so attractive is a bonus but your beauty isn't the sole attraction for me."

Damn but he had a way with words. "Then what is?"

He shook his head. "I don't know. I just know I'm smitten."

Smitten? I liked the sound of that. I smiled, pleased. "That must have been some picture she showed you."

"You were smiling into the camera wearing a dark reddish or plum colored dress that ended just below your knees in the picture she showed me. It was sleeveless and kind of highlighted your breasts and the fact that you were a woman of…substance."

"A woman of substance?"

"You weren't skinny. I'm 6' 3"and 210 lbs. The days when I found skinny women desirable are long past. These days I have no use for a skinny woman I'd be afraid of hurting when things got interesting. You looked exquisite and I was smitten."

"Smitten? You were smitten?"

"Smitten." He looked at my lips for several moments before turning in his seat to stare at the windshield again. "Completely."

"What if Jasmin had showed up instead of me?"

"I would have told her what I told her when she finally took my call today—I have zero interest in continuing any type of relationship with her. I have a feeling she would have known why—because I planned to pursue you."

I considered his words in silence for a moment. I didn't know if I believed him because it was true or because I wanted to believe him. Either way, we were ending up in bed. But I probably should show some interest in something other than his sex. "Have you ever been married?"

"No."

"Why not?"

He sighed. "Like my parents, I only planned to do it once so I didn't see any need to rush into it."

"Is there anyone special you're considering?"

He seemed to take long time to answer. "I'm not dating anyone at the moment."

"But you're sexually active?"

He turned to look at me. "I love sex but I haven't had it in several months."

*Lord he must be ripe for a night of raunchy fucking.* "Why not?"

"I'm trying to set a good example for my sons so I no longer whore around like I used to do when they were younger."

I blinked. "Jasmin never mentioned your sons."

"She doesn't know about them."

"You dated for nearly a year."

"Actually, we saw each other a few times over seven or eight months. She beat me to the punch and dumped me before I could dump her."

"And you never mentioned them to her in all that time? Not even when you gave her the bracelet?"

"Neither of us were feeling any pains when I bought it and she accepted it. I think the purchase of the bracelet is what made us wake up and realize it was time to put the brakes on our relationship. I don't want to sound as if I'm trying to diss her in any way, but we didn't spend much time getting to know each other. We had a strictly physical relationship."

Recalling how much time Jasmin had spent singing the praises of his cock, I had little reason to doubt his word.

He glanced at his watch. "It's getting late. I'll take you back to your hotel."

We made the drive back in silence. I don't know what he was thinking, but my thoughts were on wicked hot sex. My first inclination that I'd be sleeping alone came when he refused valet parking and stopped the car in one of the few pick-up spots in front of the hotel.

He walked me into the lobby and pushed the call button.

When the elevator arrived, he rode up to my suite with me. "I'll see you tomorrow for brunch—at what time?" he asked, standing just outside the door.

"You're assuming a lot," I said, annoyed that he had no intentions of spending the night with me.

"What time?" he asked again, smiling.

Damn him and that smile of his that made doing anything but what he wanted difficult. "Eleven o'clock."

He took my hand in his and kissed my palm. "I'll see you tomorrow morning at eleven."

I bit back the urge to ask him to spend the night with me. The last thing I wanted was to have him view me as a desperate, man-hungry cougar—even though that's what I felt like. "Good night."

"Sweet dreams, Shana." He bent his head to brush his warm lips against mine in a brief caress.

I leaned close and rubbed my cheek against his before turning my head to engage him in a warm, insistent lip lock.

He inhaled quickly and stepped back, shaking his head. "Don't start anything I don't have time to finish."

"Then finish it."

"I can't."

I frowned. There was no doubting the regret in his voice. So why was he leaving when he had to know I wanted him to stay. "You sound like you have another date," I teased.

"I do."

I blinked. "Excuse me?"

He stroked a finger down my cheek and neck to rest between my cleavage. "I have another date and if I don't leave now, I'll be late."

"So cancel it."

He shook his head. "That's out of the question." He bent and pressed a quick, warm kiss against the side of my neck. "Until tomorrow," he said.

I knew I was in more a long night.

He smiled and walked away.

I closed and locked the door. He had another date? Damn! What did a woman have to do to get him into bed? Entirely too wound up to sleep and worried that some lucky woman would be rocking his world that night, I undressed and had a soak until the water cooled. Then, with a hotel robe over my damp body, I poured myself a drink and went to bed.

The phone rang as I dozed off. After a moment of hesitation, I rolled over and picked it up. "Hello?"

"Hi."

At the sound of Taylor's voice, I sat up. *Please Lord, let him be calling to tell me he's cancelled his date and he's downstairs in the lobby, eager to jump my bones.* "Hi," I smiled and then frowned as I heard a series of screams. "Are you holding your date hostage?"

"That's a teen fright flick you hear. Let me go into the hall."

"A *teen* fright flick? Just how young are you and your date?"

He laughed. "I'm thirty but I'm with my sons and we're watching a movie."

"So your date was with your sons?"

"Nothing short of a date with them would have induced me to leave you."

I smiled. "A fright flick? Aren't you worried they'll have nightmares?"

"They're fourteen and fifteen and don't really do nightmares anymore."

"Fourteen and fifteen? You have sons that old?"

"I started young," he said.

"No shit, Sherlock." Not that I had much room to talk. I'd been eighteen when I got pregnant.

He laughed again. "That means I've had more time to develop my technique than other men my age."

I licked my lips. "Oh, that sounds like a promise."

"It is."

"Dad, you're missing the good parts!"

"Coming, sport." He sighed. "I have to go. My guys are calling. I'll see you tomorrow, Shana."

"I'll be waiting," I said. "Enjoy your night with your sons."

"Thanks. I always do."

Relieved that I didn't have to share him with another woman, I lay back in bed. I fell asleep quickly and slept all night.

# Chapter Three

In the morning, I took a long, relaxing soak and spent an hour preparing for our date. Since I didn't know our destination, I decided to wear a pretty, dark blue cotton-silk blend pantsuit with a pair of comfortable but dressy slip-ons.

I took extra time with my make-up and used my favorite perfume sparingly. Then satisfied I looked my best, I left my suite and went down to the lobby to wait for him. I could have waited in my suite until he arrived but I wanted to watch him walk in and be able to study him without his knowing I was.

But the moment he walked into the lobby, he immediately turned his head and looked directly at me.

Feeling like a silly, lovesick teenager, I rose and hurried across the lobby to him.

He smiled and engulfed me in a quick, warm embrace.

Strangely, I felt no awkwardness with him. Rushing into his arms seemed natural—almost as if we had a long-standing relationship that made such behavior the norm. "Shana." He kissed my ear and neck before he released me. "You look wonderful."

"So do you."

"Are you ready? Do you need to go back upstairs?"

I shook my head. "I'm all yours," I said.

"I'm going to hold you to that promise," he said, slipped an arm around my shoulders and walked me towards the door.

I enjoyed the weight of his arm around my shoulders. "Where are we going?" I asked once we were seated in his car.

"To my house for lunch. We can decide where we'll have dinner later."

"You're assuming again," I said.

Shana Mine

"And you're assuming I'm prepared to allow anyone else to monopolize your time while you're here." He turned to look at me. "For how long?"

"I'm leaving on Friday."

"So soon?"

I nodded.

"Damn. That's not much time."

It was seeming shorter with every second I spent with him.

He started the car and drove away.

He had a big two-story house forty minutes from the city. During the tour, it was clear how important his sons were to him. There was a basketball court at either end of the long driveway. The family room held a large pool table and what looked like two expensive, gaming computers as well as a large flat screen. The living room mantel held several trophies. Pictures of males on the basketball court and baseball diamonds covered the walls.

The picture hanging above the mantel featured two smiling teenage boys posing in front of a large swimming pool. They were tall with dark blond hair spilling over their shoulders. They had dark green eyes and Caucasian features but skin tones that hinted at a mixed heritage.

I turned to find Taylor standing behind me. "Your guys?"

He nodded, smiling. He pointed to the one on the right. "That's Taylor Raymond Donovan. The other is Raymond Taylor Donovan."

I arched a brow. "Unique way of naming your sons."

He shrugged. "That's as close to taking my name as their maternal grandparents would allow their mother to come. As you can imagine I was far from their favorite person after she got pregnant a second time."

"As a parent who fears the same thing, I can understand that."

"So can I," he said. "Especially now that my oldest son is the same age I was when he was conceived."

I smiled. "Your guys are stunning. You're going to have girl problems with them."

"Already started. That's why I'm trying to set a good example so neither of them becomes a father too early and finds their opportunities severely limited as I did."

"You have regrets?"

He sighed but shook his head. "I wouldn't wish either one of them unborn for a million bucks—even though I ended up in trade school instead of with the four-year degree I'd always expected to have." He bent his head and kissed my neck. "Although I'm always willing and happy to discuss my guys, right now talking isn't high on the list of things I'd love to do with you."

Smiling, I turned to face him. "That must mean food is."

He leaned close and inhaled slowly. "Damn you smell good enough to eat."

"So do you, but since I haven't had breakfast I expect some food—first."

"Food first, then I'm going to eat you," he threatened.

"Sounds like a plan."

He slipped his arm around me. "I thought we could eat by the pool."

He led me through the house and out a side door. Two tables shielded by umbrellas were on the tiles near the pool, along with several large, well-padded lounge chairs. There was also a barbeque grill, which he fired up. "I'm hoping you settle for burgers and a salad or fries."

"Sounds great," I said, slipping into the chair he held out for me. "I like mine well-done."

He brought me a glass of lemonade and some homemade garlic bread. I nibbled at the bread while watching him at the grill. He had a tight ass I looked forward to squeezing and clutching as we had sex.

"If I'd known you had a pool, I'd had brought my swimsuit with me," I said.

He turned to grin at me. "You're assuming I'd have allowed you to keep it on. And that's a false assumption. I'm one of the men who loves his women large, dark, and naked — as often as possible."

"Caveman."

"Want to be my cavewoman?"

"Hell no!"

He laughed and turned back to the grille. "You should know I'll be changing your mind."

That wouldn't take much effort — as he'd soon learn.

When the burgers were done we sat across from each other.

I ate half the salad and took a few bites of the burger before I put it down and sat staring at him.

He stared back, his food untouched.

"What kind of women do you prefer, Taylor?" I asked, pushing my plate aside. My thoughts were on his sons' obvious maternal heritage.

"Why do you ask?"

"Jasmin and I are nearly ten years your senior, plus-size, and black but your sons' mother was…"

"Their mother, Lisa, is slender with green eyes and blond hair. When I was younger I was into blondes."

"You're still young," I pointed out.

He shrugged.

"And now your preference is?"

"And now…" he rose and walked around the table.

I looked up at him. Damn he was so handsome and sexy.

He bent to kiss my neck.

I inhaled, rubbing my cheek against his. "And now?"

"And now, I'd like to be in you."

I moistened my lips. "As in?"

"I'd like to fuck you," he said.

Finally!

"How much cajoling am I going to have to do to make that happen?"

I smiled silently.

Kneeling beside me, he placed a hand on my thigh, while leaning close to nibble at my ear.

I removed his hand from my thigh and placed it inside my pants, next to my slit. "I'd like that too."

Looking in my eyes, he slipped his fingers under my thong and caressed my clit.

I bit my lip. "Oh…that feels nice." I parted my legs.

He eased his fingers into my pussy and gently finger fucked me for several delicious moments.

I closed my legs and humped myself against his fingers.

Smiling, he leaned close and kissed me.

Parting my lips, I continued to hump his fingers.

He withdrew his hand and rose. "Let's go upstairs."

Finally. I nodded and got up.

He cupped my face between his hands and pressed a long, sweet kiss against my mouth.

Feeling his tongue thrusting between my lips made me long for the same thrusting motion of his cock in my pussy. I sucked at his tongue before dragging my mouth away from his. "I can't wait to feel you inside me," I whispered.

"Then let's get this party started," he took my hand in his.

"I am so ready to do that."

We walked upstairs, hand in hand to his bedroom. He closed the door and led me over to the bed. He cupped my face in his hands and bent his head.

I closed my eyes and lifted my face.

He touched his mouth to mine in a series of quick, warm kisses before cupping one palm over my nape and slipping an arm around my waist.

I leaned closer, parting my lips and sliding my arms around him.

His arm tightened and he pressed his mouth against mine, kissing me with an insistent heat that would have melted an iceberg.

I felt his tongue gliding between my lips and in my mouth. I moaned and melted into his arms, rubbing my breasts against him.

I've always loved the intimacy that went with having sex, but what I felt for him surprised and delighted me. Even though I ached to feel his cock tunneling into my pussy, I also felt a sense of closeness I've never felt with any other man on such a sort acquaintance.

I returned his kisses, allowing him to experience my eagerness for the coming intimacy.

Taylor slid his palm from my waist into my pant bottoms. Oh hell yeah.

His hand caressing and cupping my ass sent a rush of moisture into my thong.

The long, lonely months without intercourse intensified with each touch and caress of his mouth and hands until I felt on fire. I ground my hips against his and dragged my lips from his. "Please," I whispered. "Please."

"Today is all about pleasing you," he promised.

"A handsome man who wants to please me. I like the sound of that."

"You're going to like the feel of it too."

I laughed. "I love a confident man."

"I'm very glad to hear that because I'm very confident. Now let's get you undressed so I can drink in every lovely inch of your naked body."

"Strip me, handsome."

He pressed a quick kiss against my mouth before he stepped back and quickly removed my top, revealing my bra.

With his gaze locked on my breasts, he reached out to pinch my nipples through the material.

I closed my eyes, enjoying the scent of his cologne filling my nostrils and heightening my desire.

Bending his head, he rained kisses on my cleavage and deftly unbuttoned and tossed my bra aside. After lifting his head, he stepped back to stare at my breasts.

I smiled, cupping my breasts in my palms. "You like?"

"Oh hell yeah. There's nothing as beautiful as a lovely woman with large, natural breasts."

"They'd love to meet your lips, tongue, and hands."

Slipping his arms around me, he bent to tongue and suck my breasts while he palmed and massaged my ass.

Lord that felt nice.

When he stroked a hand around my body, he pressed a finger against my clit before sliding it inside me. I arched into him and moaned with pleasure. I loved the feel of his finger inside me.

Kissing a path across to my other breast, he continued fingering me while massaging my ass.

If his fingers felt so good, I couldn't wait to feel his cock.

He brought me to the brink of orgasm before he eased his fingers out of me.

I gripped his arm. "Oh Lord Taylor, you can't stop now."

"Don't worry, sweet. I'm not stopping for long." He bent to remove my shoes before pulling my pants and thong off.

Just the way he stood staring at my naked body, as if consumed with desire, made my heart race.

"Oh damn," he said, his voice brusque. He cupped my face between his palms and kissed me until I burned for him. Then he took my hand in his and walked me over to the bed.

I lay on my back with my legs parted, my pussy wet, and aching to welcome his cock.

Kneeling at the foot of the bed, he lifted my right leg.

I sighed with pleasure when he kissed the sole of my foot.

"You have beautiful feet…hell, everything about you is beautiful," he said and then sucked each toe.

"Hmmm."

He trailed a path of warm kisses up the length of my inner thigh. "I love the feel of your skin under my lips."

The feel of his warm mouth against my slit sent chills of delight through me. I reached a hand down to curl my fingers in his long dark hair cascading over my legs. "Eat me," I pleaded.

He thrust his tongue against my clit and rained warm, moist kisses down my left inner leg to my foot. Each suck of each toe sent a rush of need through me.

I moaned. "Eat me," I begged again.

With a final suck on my big toe, he rose and started to undress.

I turned on my side to watch.

He stripped off his clothes quickly and then stood to allow me to feast on him.

Lord what a sight. Tall, muscular but not overly muscular, he had wide shoulders, a big chest, well-defined abs, and long legs. Even semi-erect, the sight of his cock made my stomach muscles clench.

I licked my lips and wiggled my hips on the bed. "Taylor..."

He stood staring at my pussy for what felt like forever before he finally rejoined me on the bed.

To my surprise, instead of positioning himself between my legs, he slid up my body and settled between my thighs with his bare, semi-erect cock pressed against my belly.

"Oh God!" I sucked in a breath and closed my eyes to more fully savor the absolutely delicious wonder of having a big, hard male body on top of me for the first time in months.

Nibbling at my neck, he rubbed his cock against my body. "You make me so hard."

Lord I was so aroused, my pussy flooded and I stroked my hands down his back to clutch his ass. I longed to reach between our bodies and stroke him until he was nice and hard and thick, and then push his bare cock deep inside me.

"What are you going to do about it?" I asked.

He turned his head and pressed his mouth against mine. His tongue slid between my lips. I dug my nails in his ass and humped against him.

In response, he reached between our bodies to grip his cock and rubbed it against my pussy.

A shudder of pleasure was overshadowed by the realization that he wore no condom, was nearly fully erect, and just inches from my pussy. Tearing my mouth from his, I pushed against his shoulders. "Taylor?"

He slid his hand up to cup my neck and recaptured my mouth, pushing his tongue between my lips.

I stiffened and struggled not to panic. He was big and strong and if he decided he wanted his bare cock inside me, I'd have a hard time trying to stop him. The realization shook me. What the hell was I doing lying naked under a man I didn't know?

Almost as if he sensed my sudden uncertainty, he lifted his mouth from mine. "No." He brushed his lips against my cheek. "It's all right, sweet. You don't ever need to be afraid of me." He lifted his head.

I opened my eyes, taking slow deep breaths.

"You don't need to worry that you'll have to fight me off or that I'll try to go raw in you. Even though I've never wanted to go raw in any woman more, I won't."

Looking into his eyes, I believed him. The tension left my body. "Thank you," I whispered.

"For what?"

"For that reassurance. I needed to hear it."

He smiled. "I have no desire or need to force any intimacy you don't want." He brushed his lips against my ear. "I want you to want me inside you."

I clutched him close again, curling my fingers in his hair. "I do want you but I don't have unsafe sex."

"Neither do I, sweet. I love my guys to death but I'm not interested in having any more kids."

"Neither am I."

"So we'll enjoy each other—safely."

"Oh yes. Please enjoy me and my pussy and let me enjoy your cock." I turned my head and kissed him.

He kissed me back, rubbing his cock against me.

I shuddered. "Put on a condom and love me," I urged.

"I'm not going to need one this time," he pulled out of my arms and kissed a wet path down my body. He rubbed his cheek against my stomach.

"Why not?" I asked, stroking my fingers through his hair.

"Because we're not having intercourse."

I stiffened. What the fuck did a woman have to do to get a fuck out of him? "What?"

He laughed. "Don't worry, sweet. I've going to make you very happy today." He trailed his tongue down my belly to the top of my slit.

I wiggled my hips. "How?"

He gently nibbled at my clit before repositioning my hips and settling down to eat me.

Oh lord. I closed my eyes and tightened my fingers in his hair.

He slipped two fingers inside my pussy. Keeping his tongue pressed against my clit, he fingered me.

Oh yeah. The long, steady pressure of his fingers thrusting in and out of me and his skillful tongue and mouth on my clit propelled me to a quick, powerful orgasm. As the tension built in the pit of my belly and exploded down to my pussy, I crushed his face against me and gushed against his lips as I came. "Ahhhh…ahhh."

He slipped his palms under my ass, tilted my hips, and licked and sucked at me as I shuddered and moaned through my climax. When my release ended, he kissed my pussy and slid up the bed to lie behind me with one hand cupping my pussy and the other splayed across my breasts.

I curled my body back against his, sighing with contentment. "Oh lord that was good."

"Glad you liked it, sweet," he murmured against my neck.

"Hmmm. What about you? You haven't come yet."

He released my pussy long enough to reach down to pull the cover up over our nude bodies before he kissed my neck. "Don't worry about me. I told you I wanted the first time to be all about you."

Touched, I turned my head to kiss him. "Thank you."

"My pleasure, sweet."

I closed my eyes. After a few minutes lying in his embrace to savor the afterglow of my climax, I was going to pleasure him. Either we'd have intercourse or I'd suck his cock or both.

* * *

I woke later to feel warm lips caressing mine. When I opened my eyes, Taylor, fully dressed and looking freshly showered, sat on the side of the bed. He smiled and caressed my cheek. "I've washed your underwear and there's a new toothbrush in the bathroom, along with a warm bath waiting for you."

I stroked a hand down his cheek. "You're too good to be true."

He shook his head. "No. I'm not. What you see is what you'll get."

A thoughtful lover considerate enough to wash my underwear and run a bath all before he's sought any sexual satisfaction for himself. Clearly, I'd died and gone to heaven. "Where have you been all my life?"

"I'm here now," he said, kissed my lips and rose. "You don't want your water to cool. Everything you need is in the bathroom, including an mp3 player with over five hundred of my favorite songs. Hopefully there's something you'll like." He pointed to an open door across the room. "The bathroom is through that door, sweet."

Feeling at ease with him, I slipped out of bed and walked towards the bathroom.

He let out a low wolf whistle.

Smiling, I blew him a kiss over my shoulder before continuing through the open doorway.

The bathroom had a large shower with frosted doors and a modern tub with jets and soft, recessed lights surrounding the tub. A heated towel rack stood at one end of the tub.

Taking a moment to choose from a collection of bath salts, I added them and slipped into the tub. I found some jazz I liked, put in the ear buds, and lay back until the cooling water roused me.

After drying off, I wrapped a towel around my body and went back into the bedroom.

Taylor had made the bed and my freshly laundered underwear lay in the middle, along with my shoulder bag. My clothing lay across the bedrail.

Smiling at his consideration, I dressed, and made up my face. Then I went downstairs. Following the sound of jazz, I found Taylor seated in the living room.

He immediately rose and crossed the room to kiss my cheek. "Have dinner with me?"

I put my arm around his waist and smiled at him. "I'd love to."

He hugged me and walked me over to the loveseat. Seating me, he crossed the room to the bar. "Would you like a drink?"

What I wanted was to spend the night in bed with his hard cock thrusting deep in and out of my pussy. I shook my head. "No thanks."

He returned to sit beside me, placing arm along the back of the loveseat. "Tell me about your marriage."

"My ex and I grew apart, but we've remained civil for the sake of our kids."

"Did you love him?"

"Yes. He was my first love and I was his but we married so young that when we grew up we realized we had very little in common. Still, the divorce was difficult for me to deal with for a long time because he was the only man I'd ever loved."

"What happened between you and your sons' mother? Didn't you want to marry her?"

"Not really, but her parents pressured me and I would have caved and married her but my parents wouldn't give their consent."

"And when you were old enough to marry on your own?"

"I no longer imagined myself in love and I was enjoying the mystique women like to weave around Native American males and sleeping with everyone in sight. I only slowed down a few years ago when my sons started to develop an interest in girls. I don't want them to make the mistakes I've made so I'm trying to set a good example."

"How do they react when they meet your women?"

"They've never met any of them."

That surprised me. "None?"

"None. I can't see any point in confusing them by introducing them to women who are just a means to an end."

"That's cold."

"You asked and I'm being honest. I've never been interested enough in any woman to bring her into my guys' lives."

"But you've had a lot women in your life?"

"Yes. I like women and they like me so we often ended up in bed." He squeezed my shoulders. "What about you and men after your divorce?"

"There were only two. The last one dumped me after three years."

"No shit. Recently?"

"Yes. It happened just over six months ago."

"Did you love him?"

"No, but I was damned fond of him."

"I'm selfishly glad it didn't work out between you two."

I smiled and leaned back against him. "So am I—now that's we've met."

He glanced at his watch. "Where would you like to have dinner?"

"Some place where we can dance."

"And after dinner?" He brushed his fingers against the side of my neck. "Will you spend the night with me?"

I hesitated, recalling those brief moments earlier when I'd panicked because I wasn't sure of him. Then I remembered how quickly he'd reassured me. Sleeping with a man I'd only known for a day was sheer madness. But despite our cultural and age differences, there was something about being with Taylor that had felt right. I'd been aware of it from the moment we met. Each moment spent with him intensified that certainty.

"Oh hell yeah," I said again.

"I spend Wednesday nights with my guys, but I'm hoping you'll consider spending the other nights you're here with me."

Considering how I was already feeling, I knew that probably wouldn't be a good idea. Nevertheless the thought of spending a night alone that I could spend with him didn't make sense. I'd be back in San Francisco soon enough and I didn't intend to have any regrets for not having made the most of the short amount of time we had together. "I'll consider it," I said.

He bent his head to muzzle my neck. "How long do I have to help you make the decision?"

I placed a hand over his hair. "If you keep this up, I'll make it right now," I said.

He laughed and lifted his head to smile at me. "Do you have any idea how sexy you are?"

"I'm glad you think so."

"How could I not?" He lifted my hand to his lips and kissed it. "Would you like to put me out of my misery and let me take you back to your hotel to get your luggage before we go out to dinner?"

I stared at him. He was young, handsome, and clearly found me attractive. The powerful attraction was mutual. Why should I waste time pretending otherwise? "Yes. Our next time together will be all about you," I promised as I leaned close to kiss his warm, firm lips.

He leaned away from me. "Don't start anything you're not prepared to finish right now," he warned.

"Who says I'm not ready to finish it?" I demanded.

He inhaled slowly before shaking his head and rising. "Let's go get your luggage and head out to dinner. Then the night will be all ours."

"Sounds like a plan."

After picking up my luggage from the hotel, we had dinner in Chinatown.

"Are you dating anyone?" he asked.

I shook my head. "I had just starting thinking about dating again when Jasmin asked me to come here to see you."

"I'm glad she decided to dump me before I could dump her."

"Or we wouldn't have met?"

He arched a brow.

"What?"

He shook his head. "I told you I was smitten the moment I saw you. And you should know that I haven't slept with anyone since I saw your picture."

"I'm touched," I said.

"You're going to be fucked," he countered.

"You say that like it's a bad thing."

He laughed. "Would you like anything else?"

*Just you buried deep inside me.* "No."

We drove along the Benjamin Franklin Parkway and took pictures in front of the Rocky statue at the foot of the Philadelphia Museum of Art. I was surprised to see so many couples sitting on the steps.

We joined them to enjoy the beauty of the starlit night. He sat two steps above me with his arms around me. Leaning back against him while staring up at the stars, a feeling that had very little to do with passion overwhelmed me. Within the circle of his arms, I knew I wanted more from him than a few short days and nights of passion. I wanted to get to know him and have our lives intertwined.

Shaken by the realization, I turned my head to look at him.

He met my gaze, a slow smile spreading across his handsome face.

"It's a beautiful night," I said.

"Being with you makes it even more beautiful," he responded.

*And you are so handsome and sexy, being with you is like winning the lottery.*

We remained on the steps for another twenty minutes before we decided to leave. We walked to his car, hand in hand. On the drive back to his house, he stopped at a convenience store to buy me a bouquet of flowers and a ridiculously expensive red and white teddy bear with *I heart you* on its chest.

I stared at the bear and then up at him as he finished paying for it.

He arched a brow and then gave me one of those slow, sexy smiles of his that made me burn for him. I couldn't deny the powerful attraction I felt for him.

# Chapter Four

At his house, he poured me a drink and then went to carry my suitcase up to his bedroom. I turned out the lights and stood in front of the large windows, staring up at the moonlit sky.

When he returned to the living room, I put my untouched drink down and walked across the room to him. I reached behind him to release his hair so it fell across his shoulders. Then I linked my arms around his neck. "It's your turn," I whispered, lifting my mouth for a kiss.

He engulfed me in his arms and bent to kiss me with a fierce intensity I felt all through my body.

I responded with a passion I knew signified my willingness and desire to rock his world that night.

His big hands caressing and massaging my ass set me on fire.

I curled my fingers in his hair and reached between our bodies to rub my hand against his hardening cock. "I want to feel you deep inside me...filling me up."

He slipped his hands in my pants and slapped each cheek while he sucked hard at my neck.

I knew he intentionally wanted to leave a hickey and the thought sent a thrill through me. I clutched his head close as he continued to suck at my neck. "Brand me, baby," I encouraged.

When he finally lifted his head, my thong was flooded and I was on fire with the need to feel him inside me.

I leaned against him, my heart racing. "I need to feel you inside me."

Smiling, he reclaimed my mouth, thrusting his tongue inside.

I moaned against his lips rubbing myself against his hard cock.

He gently lowered me onto the carpet, his mouth never leaving my hungry one.

I welcomed the weight of his big body onto mine. I slipped my arms around his broad shoulders and clung to him, parting my legs so he could slip between my thighs. Lord he felt so good.

We lay kissing and grinding against each other until I unzipped his pants and pushed my fingers inside to curl around his cock.

He was hard and fully aroused and I ached to feel him sliding in me. I tore my mouth from his. I eagerly massaged and pumped him. "Condoms," I whispered, easing his hard length out of his pants.

He groaned and moved off me. Reaching in his pocket, he pulled out his wallet and quickly rolled it over himself.

I sat on my haunches, staring at him. I was only seconds away from feeling his big, hard shaft powering into my body. He was longer and thicker than all my other lovers.

Mindlessly, I reached my hands out to cup his balls in one hand and pumped him with my other.

He leaned close to whisper in my ear. "Are you just going to pump me all night or would you like to feel my dick in your pussy?"

Feverish to be fucked, I stood up and started undressing.

He rose too and we tore at each other's clothes until we were both naked. Devoid of clothes, we fell back onto the floor together in a tangle of arms and legs rubbing against each other.

I turned onto my back and reached for him. "Taylor...Taylor..."

He sprawled on his stomach and licked and nibbled at my slit, making me wetter and hotter.

"No...no." I wiggled my hips. "I need you inside me."

He spent several more moments eating my pussy before he finally kissed his way up my trembling body and slipped between my thighs, resting his weight on his extended arms.

At the feel of his big, hard body, pressing down onto mine, I shivered with need. "Please!" I whispered, reaching between our bodies to grip his cock. I rubbed it along my slit. "Love me."

He stared down at me, his eyes dark with desire. "I should make love to you our first time, but I'm afraid I'm going to have to fuck you instead."

"Oh baby! That's what I want," I told him. "Let the fucking begin—now!" I gripped his lean hips and jerked down on them while I thrust mine off the carpet. And oh lord I nearly meowed like an alley cat as I felt his long, hard, thick cock pushing up into my wet, aching pussy.

He slid in quick and deep, filling me as no other man ever had.

For a moment, we lay still, staring into each other's eyes and enjoying the sheer beauty of having his cock locked inside my pussy. I felt so full.

Then he groaned and shoved his hips forward.

I shuddered and gasped in delighted surprised as the movement sent another delicious inch or two of cock inside me. "Oh God, you're big and hard."

He smiled. "A big, hard dick makes for a deep, pussy-pleasing fuck for you, my sweet," he whispered.

"I've never had such a big cock inside me," I admitted, aware my voice was full of lust.

"And I've never had the pleasure of being inside a sweeter pussy." He shuddered suddenly. "Oh damn sweet, I've never felt like this with anyone else."

"Neither have I," I moaned, tightening myself around him.

"Oh damn your pussy feels good," he said. "I've wanted to fuck you from the moment I saw your picture."

With that sweet admission filling my senses, I slapped his ass cheeks hard. "Then fuck me, my big, handsome hunk."

He withdrew his hips until nearly half his cock was outside my body. Then he slowly pushed his entire length balls deep inside me again.

"Oh yes! Yes!"

He did that several times, making my body arch, my toes curl, and my nipples harden.

Tired of being teased, I linked my legs over his hips and gripped his tight ass, forcing his cock back inside my pussy.

He groaned and pushed and pulled his cock in and out of me in rapid succession.

Lord the jolts of pleasure I felt with each thrust were nearly off the charts.

Digging my nails in his ass, I ground myself against him.

He paused and then stroked deep into me again.

It took a few moments before we found the perfect rhythm. Once we had, we sucked each other's tongues and moved together in a wild, intimate dance that took us both quickly to new heights. He fucked me so hard and deep that my inner thighs shook and he started to inflict the most exquisite pleasure imaginable on me.

Drowning in a wave of joy, I cried out, raked my nails over his tight, clenching ass, and came all over the most wonderful cock I'd ever had the pleasure of having fuck the hell out of me.

He clutched me closer and fucked me harder.

Lord I thought I would lose my mind as I came again and lost control of everything and then happily floated away on a cloud of pure, white hot mental and sexual satisfaction.

When I came back to my senses, I lay on my back with my legs parted.

He propped himself up on one elbow, staring down at me with a look of concern on his face. "Shana, are you all right? Did I hurt you?"

Shana Mine

I nodded and then smiled. "Lord yes, you did and I loved every second of it," I told him. Sighing with remembered pleasure, I reached down to close my fingers around his cock. He'd removed the condom but was still semi-aroused. "Every fucking second and I do mean fucking, Taylor."

He laughed and leaned down to press a moist kiss against my mouth. "That's what I'm talking about, an honest and passionate woman. What more could a man want?"

I felt his fingers stroking into my pussy. I shuddered, turning my head to kiss his neck. "Lord your technique is out of this world, Taylor. I swear that was the best fuck I've ever had."

"Me too," he said. "And just so you know, sweet, a dick is only as good as the superb pussy it's inside—especially when it's dispensing the level of pleasure you gave me. I've never felt any pussy as good as yours and I've had lots of pussy." He shook his head. "But I don't want you to think that what we just shared was all about sex for me, Shana. It wasn't."

Touched that he'd also felt more than a physical connection, I pulled him down on top of me and kissed his neck. "Thank you for telling me that."

"It's the truth, Shana."

"For me too, Taylor."

He turned us on our sides where we lay holding each other for several minutes in silence before he sighed and sat up. "You know what I'd like?"

"Another fuck?" I asked hopefully.

He laughed. "Yes, but I was thinking how much I'd like to take a bath with you."

"Sounds like a plan." I stretched out my hands.

He clasped them in his and pulled me to my feet.

We picked up our clothes and went upstairs to the master bathroom.

He turned on the faucets.

Ignoring his frown, I added salts and slipped into the slick, warm water.

"The water's perfect. Come join me, handsome."

"In a moment." He left the bathroom. When he returned, he had a bottle of wine and two glasses. Placing them on the tub apron, he slipped in the bath, facing me.

I watched as he filled the glasses and handed me one.

He lifted his, smiling at me. "To the most beautiful, sexy woman I've ever had the pleasure to meet."

I loved his smile and that he did it so often. "To the handsome hunk who's touched my emotions in a way no other man has on such short acquaintance."

We touched our glasses and locked gazes as we drank our wine.

He finished his and lay back in the tub. "Come lie in my arms, sweet."

"Gladly," I said. Putting my glass on the apron, I stretched out on top of him with my back pressed against his front.

He slipped his arms around me and stroked two fingers in my pussy.

I leaned back against him. "I'm feeling so mellow right now I'm almost afraid that this is a sweet dream."

He stroked his free hand over my breasts. "I know the feeling, sweet."

"I love how I feel when you touch my naked flesh."

"I love it too," he said against my hair.

"This is the perfect night and I wish it could last forever."

"Me too," he kissed my hair.

Smiling, I closed my eyes and allowed the soothing motion of the water jets and his hands to lull me to sleep.

He woke me later. "Let's go to bed."

I nodded, still feeling drowsy.

After getting out of the tub, he offered me a hand to help me out.

Shana Mine

We dried each other off and then tumbled into bed and into each other's arms.

He rolled me onto my back and slipped between my legs. "Oh sweet, I ache for you."

I held him close, running my fingers through his long, dark hair. "I'm yours for the taking, Taylor. Take me as often as you want."

He spent several minutes kissing me before he rolled over to reach for a condom from the top drawer of his nightstand.

Taking the pack from him, I tore the top off before I paused.

"What's wrong?" he asked.

"Nothing. I just I want to taste you." I felt my cheeks burning at the admission.

He met my gaze. "Do you?"

I bit my lip, confused by the intensity of his gaze—almost as if he knew I generally disliked having a man's cock anywhere near my mouth. "Taste…not suck," I said quickly.

"Understood, sweet. At the moment, I'm more interested in your pussy than I am in having you suck my cock. Taste away and get it out of your system so I can make love to you."

I'd reluctantly sucked my ex's cock because he enjoyed it but I'd hated every second of having his big cock inside my mouth. Taylor was bigger and thicker. Sucking him was not on my list of immediate things to do but my desire to even taste his cock shocked me.

I moistened my lips and knelt between his legs. Cupping his big balls in one hand, I extended my tongue and licked the underside of his length. As I did, I inhaled slowly, enjoying the aroma of his cock.

I licked and nibbled at the base of his shaft several times before I took a deep breath and sucked the big head of his cock between my lips.

Although he groaned with pleasure, he made no effort to cup his hands over my head or to push more of himself into my mouth. He allowed me to control how much of his shaft I drew into my mouth and how much I sucked him before I sat back on my heels. When I did, he was deliciously hard and thick.

He immediately slipped the condom on and lay on his back, drawing me down on top of him. "Fuck me, sweet."

"Gladly," I whispered, lifted my hips, and slowly sank down on his cock. "Oh…" I moaned at the feel of the big head parting my slit and sliding deep into my pussy. "Oh lord." I shuddered and ground my hips against his. "The only way this could get better is with your bare cock in me."

He stiffened under me. "We can't do that."

I nodded. "I know. I know, but a woman can fantasize. Can't she?"

"Yes. I like the idea that you might fantasize about me. God knows I've been doing it about you since I saw your picture."

"Ditto, handsome."

"Ditto what?"

"I've been daydreaming about you before we even met," I said, kissed his lips, and sat up. Keeping his shaft in me, I placed my hands on his chest.

"Damn. If I'd known that, I'd have been to San Francisco in a heartbeat looking for you."

Smiling with satisfaction at the admission, I rode him slowly. I loved the feel of his thick, heavy shaft sliding in and out of me.

"Damn Shana, you feel so good." He reached up to pinch my nipples and massage my breasts as he pushed his hips off the bed, driving himself deep inside me.

I closed my eyes and increased the motion of my hips. There was nothing in the world as good as the feel of his hard shaft sliding in and out of me, sending waves of pleasure through my body like jolts of sensual electricity. The emotional connection I felt with him bolstered the joy and delight of having our bodies joined as one.

As the passion and sexual tension built between us, he slid his hands down my back to my ass. Taking control of our fuck, he slapped my cheeks each time he shoved his hips up, driving his cock as deep in my body as possible.

Lord. Oh lord. What incredible feelings rushed through me when my orgasm roared through me. While I was still drowning in absolute waves of pleasure, he turned me onto my back, lifted his weight onto his extended arms, and stroked in and out of my pussy with deep, steady strokes that quickly drove him to his orgasm.

I loved how he groaned and lowered his big body onto mine, shivering and whispering almost incoherently.

I slipped my arms around him and held him close.

He crushed me under him for several moments before he turned on his side to remove his condom and toss it in the trashcan beside the bed. Then he rolled back into my waiting arms.

I kissed him and curled my fingers in his hair.

"Hell, that was incredibly good," he said.

"Totally," I agreed.

"Yeah?" He lifted his head to smile down at me.

"Hell to the yeah."

"Want to do it again?"

"Abso-fucking-lutely."

He laughed and sank his teeth into my right breast.

I reached down to slap his ass. And it was on again.

We made love late into the night before he curled his body against my back and we lay together spoon style. All of my lovers—including my ex—had rolled away after sex and fallen asleep on the other side of the bed. I loved that Taylor wanted to maintain physical contact even after he'd come. In a word, I fell asleep thinking that he was perfect. Jasmin had been right. He was the complete package.

\* \* \*

In the morning, we shared a hard, quick fuck, during which he made me feel as if he couldn't keep those big, warm, calloused hands of his off me. He whispered that I was sexy and beautiful and he was going to make me his.

Hell, that wouldn't take much effort, I thought as we walked into the master bath to shower together.

Afterwards, he dressed quickly and then slowly toweled my body. He then spread my favorite lotion all over my body. Then I took over and slipped on a new dark pink swimming suit that I knew flattered me.

We had breakfast out by the pool. After coffee, we dozed in the warmth of the morning sun. When we woke, we had a quick swim and then spread several towels on the grass along one side of the pool. I straddled his hips and slowly pushed my hips forward, allowing his big dick to ease up inside me.

"Shit," he said, gripping my hips. "You feel good."

"So do you," I told him.

We had a quick, raunchy fuck.

By the time it was over, my breasts felt sore from his vigorous sucking and my ass stung from the sensual paddling from his big hands. Our release was swift and powerful. Surfacing from another climax, I climbed off his cock and rolled onto my stomach. "Oh damn. If we keep this up, you'll stretch my pussy out of shape for all other guys," I teased.

To my surprise, he slapped each of my naked ass cheeks so hard they stung. "Hey!" I sat up and stared at him. "That hurt."

He narrowed his dark gaze and gave me a cool look. "I won't talk to you about fucking other women so don't you talk to me about letting other men fuck you! That's the last thing I want to hear from you."

I blinked, shocked both by his slapping my ass so hard and the vehemence in his voice and eyes. I compressed my lips and tried to keep my voice level when I responded. "Unless we're having sex, you don't get to hit my ass that hard, Taylor. That hurt and I'm not taking that shit from any man."

"Do I look like I have any damned interest in hearing how you plan to let other men fuck you, Shana?"

"What's wrong with you?" I shook my head, some of my anger evaporating. "That remark was meant as a compliment, Taylor."

He stared at me in silence before he slowly inhaled and exhaled. "Fuck! I had no right to slap your ass that hard."

"Why did you?"

He shook his head. "Jealousy, but that's no excuse. I'm sorry. Please forgive me."

I sighed, uncertain how to respond. Did he have a temper or a tendency to think he had the right to hit a woman when he was angry?

As before, he seemed to almost know what I was thinking. "I don't hit women."

I bit back the urge to ask why he'd made an exception in my case. In all honesty, I didn't consider that he'd hit me. After all, we'd just finished having sex and I'd only climbed off his cock moments before.

"I promise you that won't happen again, Shana."

"Why did it happen at all?"

He sighed. "You…I…I haven't felt so…drawn to a woman in a very long time. Being with you has unnerved me. I promise you I've never manhandled a woman and I sure as well don't intend to start with you, sweet. It will not happen again."

"I'll hold you to that promise and I will not excuse your slapping my ass like that again," I warned. "Slapping it hard during sex is one thing. What you just did is another one."

"You have my word it won't ever happen again."

I nodded, dismayed to feel my throat tightening up as I accepted his word. Then I realized I was close to tears because he didn't need to keep his promise for long. In five days, I'd be on a plane heading home, leaving him behind.

I closed my eyes and lay on my belly, burying my face in my arms.

He leaned over and kissed my shoulder. "Please don't cry, sweet. There's no need. I promise."

I bit my lip and breathed slowly. "I believe you," I said, when I could trust my voice.

He kissed my neck and then lifted me up and engulfed me in his arms. "Oh God, Shana."

Oh God, what? I drew back to look at him.

He glanced away and released me. "Do you want to have dinner out?"

I shook my head. I wanted to spend as much of the next five days alone with him as possible. "I want to be alone with you and have you fuck me senseless as often as possible," I admitted. "Each moment you're not inside me is going to be a moment wasted."

"You sound like a woman falling in love."

Oh hell no! I couldn't afford to allow that to happen. After having felt his cock branding my pussy as his alone, I knew there was no way in hell Jasmin wouldn't want him back when she returned.

"You sound like a man who'd like that to be true," I countered.

He nodded. "Who can blame me? You're a beautiful woman…an exquisite lover and I'm totally smitten with you." He caressed my cheek. "Everything about you from the tone of your beautiful skin to every inch of your sexy body and seductive voice excite me. I look at you and I'm lost and don't want to be found."

My heart raced with excitement at his words. "I'm nine years older than you and my son is only ten years younger than you," I said.

"Do I look like I care about that or any other nonsense reason you might come up with to try to keep us apart?"

"No, but you're probably allowing that big, beautiful cock of yours to do your talking."

"What the fuck!" He exploded to his feet and glared down at me. "You think I'm just a big cock without a mind of my own? Fuck you!"

I stared in shocked as he stormed into the house, sliding the patio door shut so hard that I was amazed the glass didn't shatter.

No doubt about it. He had quite a temper. Picking up my clothes, I dressed slowly before I walked into the empty living room.

After a moment's hesitation, I decided it might be best to allow him some time to cool off before I went in search of him. I took the time to study the many pictures in the room. One I hadn't noticed before was of Taylor and a man who looked so much like him that he had to be his father. He appeared to be in his early fifties. The long dark hair draped over his shoulders held no hint of gray.

They were both on horseback and smiling into the camera as they posed along a wooded trail. I smiled, realizing Taylor would probably look much like his handsome father in another twenty-five years or so.

*Not that it will be any of your business what he'll look like then,*
I reminded myself and turned away from the picture. Next to
it was a picture of Taylor's father with his arm around a pretty
woman with long dark hair who must be his mother. Small
wonder Taylor was so tall. His mother looked as if she were
close to six feet.

Sighing with regret for all the reasons he and I wouldn't
have a relationship after the coming Friday, I left the room.

Following the sounds of a bouncing basketball, I went out
to the driveway. Wearing a pair of dark shorts, he ran down
the driveway and sank the ball into the hoop. He stopped
when he saw me.

I gave him my full attention.

He stared at me, tossing the ball aside. "If you're expecting
me to apologize, don't hold your breath."

"That makes a lot of sense."

He narrowed his gaze and stalked along the driveway to
glare down at me." If I'm behaving irrationally, it's because
you're driving me nuts."

I arched a brow. "And here I thought because you were
old enough to make love, you were also old enough to be
responsible for your own actions. My bad."

He stared at me and then abruptly laughed.

I laughed too, relieved.

He reached out to embrace me.

I slipped my arms around him.

In response, he kissed my ear. "Oh, sweet. I want you so
much I feel as if I'm being consumed."

I turned my head and kissed his lips. "Then take me. Fuck
me. Spank my ass as hard as you like—during sex or
foreplay."

"I want to fuck it," he said, sliding his palms down to cup my nether cheeks. "Long and hard until you come so hard you scream the house down—and then I want to fuck you some more until you'll never even think of allowing any other man near this pussy because it's mine, Shana!"

The thought of his hard cock forcing its way into my ass sent waves of pure, unadulterated lust flowing through every vein in my body. But having anal sex with him so soon after meeting him would make me feel like one of the naughty, nasty girls my mother had taught me never to be. "Taylor—"

"It's my pussy." He shocked me by slipping his hand into my pants and inserting his fingers inside me in the middle of his driveway in broad daylight. While the pool area was shielded from possible prying eyes, the driveway wasn't.

"Taylor!" I slapped at his hand and quickly stepped back.

He pulled me close again and thrust his fingers back inside me. "Who does this wet, tight pussy belong to?" he demanded, bending to kiss me.

I shuddered as he finger fucked me. "It's yours, Taylor. All yours," I moaned and finally pulled away, pushing his fingers out of me. I didn't dare look around—afraid I'd see one of his neighbors watching.

"That's what I thought." He slipped an arm around my shoulders and walked me back inside.

I pushed his arm off my shoulders. "That doesn't mean you should finger fuck me in the driveway!"

"You're right but it's difficult to make rational choices when I'm with you."

Who could stay angry after a remark like that?

Clearly aware that I was no longer angry with him, he kissed my lips before he led me upstairs.

In his bedroom, I did a slow striptease for him while he sat in one of the chairs by the window, watching and massaging himself.

"What do you think?" I asked, standing nude in front of him.

He extended a hand. "I think you should come over here so we can rock each other's world."

"I love a man with a plan," I said. Pinching my nipples, I walked over to the chair as he rose. "What do you have in mind?"

He caressed my cheek. "Branding you as mine."

"So what are you waiting for?"

He turned the chair around and bent me over it.

I immediately knew what he had in mind and I couldn't wait.

Standing behind me, he rained moist kisses on my neck and shoulders before he straightened.

I glanced over my shoulder and deliberately licked my lips. "I'm all yours, Taylor. Take me."

He caressed each ass cheek, bent to kiss them and then slowly spanked and paddled my ass until it burned and I shook with need. "My ass is yours," I whispered. "Take it."

He leaned over me to kiss my neck and pinch my nipples. "I'm going to, but it might be a little uncomfortable."

"It's a chance I'm willing to take," I assured him.

He released me and stood up.

Keeping my eyes closed, I listened to the sound of him tearing open a condom.

"Show me you want this too, sweet. Part your cheeks for me."

I reached back to spread my cheeks for him.

"Oh damn Shana, you have a lovely, lovely ass."

"And it's all yours, handsome."

He eased the head of the tube between my cheeks and squeezed some into me. My heart raced as he then gently pushed a single, lubed finger into me.

I really had to be into a partner to even begin to enjoy anal sex. I was so into Taylor, I knew the neighbors would probably hear me moaning when he plugged my ass with his long, thick, hard cock.

My pussy flooded at the thought.

Gently sliding a second finger into my rectum, he rained hot, biting kisses against my ear, neck, and shoulders.

I reached for his other hand and pushed it between my legs and inside me. "Oh…" I moaned. "Oh lord. I need you inside me, baby."

He bit my ear. "Where do you want me, sweet?"

I shuddered. "In my ass," I whispered. "Deep in my ass. It's burning for you—just as my pussy does."

As his warm, triumphant laughter filled my ears, he withdrew his fingers from both my front and my rear.

I turned to see him massaging his cock. "Hey, you gonna play with yourself or are you going to take care of business?" I released my ass cheeks.

He smiled but made no move to slide that big, lubed shaft of his into me.

"That's a big cock you're packing. If you keep me waiting too much longer, I'll come to my senses and realize you're too big to be in my ass."

"Fuck that. Spread those luscious dark cheeks of your for me again, my sweet Shana."

Trembling with anticipation, I reached back to hold my cheeks apart, exposing my anus. "Take it," I whispered, burning with desire. "Like my pussy, it's all yours, baby."

He slapped and paddled each cheek again, making them burn.

Every hard contact of his hand on my naked flesh caused shocks of delight to dance through my body.

When I could bear the tension no longer, I moaned.

In response, he gripped one of my hips and positioned his cockhead against my ass.

I tensed and waited for that first painful push.

"Slide your cheeks back until you drive my dick inside," he whispered.

Taking a quick breath, I obeyed. After pushing my hips backward with a steady pressure for a few moments, I froze.

"Keep coming, sweet," he encouraged. "Keep coming and let me claim your ass."

Sinking my teeth into my bottom lip, I gingerly eased back until I felt his hard cockhead pressing against me. Then I shook and froze.

He kissed my neck. "If you're not ready for this, I can wait."

The whispered assurance dispelled enough of my tension to allow me to push backward until his cockhead slid into my anal entrance.

"Fuck!" he groaned, leaning over my back to cup my breasts in his palms. "Don't stop now."

Gasping for breath, I shoved backwards, allowing his big cock to slip up into my ass. Feeling him stretching me, I froze and moaned with the discomfort of having even a quarter of his thickness in me. "Don't thrust, Taylor or you'll destroy my ass," I warned. "Don't thrust."

"Oh shit." He kissed my neck. "Of course I'm going to thrust." Sliding one hand down from my breasts, he rubbed against my clit and gently started drawing his cock out until only the head remained inside me.

"Don't thrust," I whispered, even as my body burned for him to thrust deep and hard until he hurt me. I wanted my ass to burn with a fire that only he could extinguish.

Slipping two fingers inside my pussy, he pushed his cock back inside, driving it in deeper.

I gasped and shuddered, so filled with lust I couldn't think of anything but the big, hard weapon about to totally destroy my ass. Oh fuck, I was hot for it to happen.

When he had half his length buried in my stretched ass, he sucked the side of my neck and fingered my pussy as he started a slow, sensual sliding motion in and out of me.

Consumed with need and greedy for the combination of pleasure and pain I now hungered for, I gritted my teeth and forced my ass backward, driving most of his cock inside.

He stroked in deeper.

"Oh God!" I sobbed, my entire body shaking.

To my surprise, he froze and brushed his lips against my ear. "Do you want me to stop, sweet? We don't have to do this if it's too painful for you."

I released my ass cheeks and reached back to grip his hips, pulling them closer. "It hurts like hell, but I want more. I want every inch burning my ass and setting it on fire," I moaned. "It's your ass. Take it. Fuck it. Use it any way you like. Just don't stop."

After several moments of hesitation, he gripped my hips, leaned over to kiss the corner of my mouth, and fucked nearly all of his cock deep in my ass.

I sank my teeth into my bottom lip to keep from crying out.

Rotating his powerful hips, he fucked my ass with long, deep, measured thrusts that sent chills of pain, tinged with the most delicious pleasure through me.

As he drilled my ass with a ruthless precision that I loved, he finger fucked my pussy and rubbed his thumb against my clit. And whispered to me in what I assumed was his native tongue.

I didn't know what he was saying and didn't care. I just wanted those hard, deep plunges to continue in my ass. Conversely, the more painful his fucking became, the more I enjoyed it and the closer he seemed.

When I felt the tension building in his big body and knew he was about to come, I gritted my teeth and recklessly pushed my hips back to meet his pistoning cock.

I didn't expect to come but when he abruptly drove his entire shaft as deep in my ass as he could when he came, I gasped and shuddered. Then I felt the most incredible orgasm of my life rush over me and totally consume me.

Collapsing against the chair back, I sobbed with pleasure, my whole body shaking with the force of my release.

He kept his entire cock buried deep in my burning, aching ass as he groaned in my ear until he finally stopped coming.

"Oh…Taylor."

He kissed my neck, eased his cock out of me, discarded the condom, and turned me into his arms.

I leaned against him, feeling limp.

# Chapter Five

Together, we stumbled over to the bed and fell in it. We lay trembling for several minutes before he rolled onto his back and drew my body on top of his. "Damn. I've never felt anything anywhere near as good as that," he whispered. He stroked his hands over my ass. "Are you all right, sweet? I know that was painful."

"Painful isn't a strong enough word, but damn I loved it," I admitted. "I loved it, Taylor." *And I think I'm on my way to loving you.*

He hugged me close. "I don't like the thought of hurting you during sex."

I sighed. "These last few days have been an eye-opener. I used to wonder how any woman could possibly enjoy painful sex. Now I know how — with the right man any sexual experience can be fulfilling and enjoyable."

"And I'm the right man?"

"Oh, yes." I sighed. "There's a very thin line between pleasure and pain and damn but you cross it so skillfully, Taylor. I've never been with any other man who fucked or made love as skillfully as you do. I get chills just thinking of your cock pushing inside me and branding my pussy and my ass as your exclusive property."

He whispered to me again.

"What language is that and what did you say?" I asked.

"It's Tsalagi, my mother's native tongue."

"That's Cherokee. Isn't it?"

"Yes."

"And your father? Doesn't he speak Tsalagi?"

"My father is Apache, but he was raised with English as his native tongue. Over the years, he's learned to speak Tsalagi, after a fashion, to please my mother."

"What were you saying when you spoke Tsalagi?"

"Nothing of great importance."

"Then tell me."

"You can't hold a man to things said in the heat of passion, Shana."

What the hell had he said? "What can't I hold you to, Taylor?"

He sighed. "You make me burn like no other woman ever has. I might have mentioned feeling as if I'm in danger of developing an obsession with you."

I lifted up and looked down at him. "Did you say anything about love in your native tongue?"

He lowered his lids to conceal his expression. "I might have, but then I don't know much about romantic love because I've never really felt it."

"What about your guys' mother?"

"I was in lust with her and I had and have a deep affection for her."

"Have?"

"She's the mother of my sons. Her parents wanted her to abort them but she wouldn't. She's a great mother and I'll always have some warm feelings for her because of my guys, but I've never really loved her or anyone else."

"Have you mentioned love to any other woman during sex?"

"It wasn't just sex and no I haven't," he said shortly. "But don't read anything into that admission, Shana."

I rolled away from him. "Heaven forbid I should flatter myself into thinking that my pussy and ass are so divine, they made you fall in love with me."

He laughed and followed me, curling his body against mine. "Actually, they are that good," he whispered.

"Are you saying you're in love—"

"I'm not saying anything except that we tend to think with our cocks and a couple of good fucks can send some men tumbling head over heels in love."

Shana Mine

I turned in his arms to face him. "But not you?"

He shrugged, rolling onto his back. "I don't have a clear enough head to know what I'm feeling right now. I just know it's powerful and I've never felt it before."

"And?" I pressed.

"And I like it...hell, I love it. I want some more of it and of you."

"I want that too." I sighed. "We have five days to explore how we feel."

"And then?"

"And then I'm going home and I'm taking my heart with me."

"I wouldn't count on that if I were you. I have your pussy and your ass. What makes you think I'll allow you to keep your heart?"

"Because it's not up for grabs," I said turning onto my side.

"If I decide I want it, I'll take it," he said in a cool, determined voice. "Just as I took the rest of your delectable body." He put an arm around me and drew me back against his body.

I went willingly, molding my ass to his groin.

"You're mine," he said and clutched me closer with a possessiveness I had to admit I enjoyed.

"For now," I teased.

"Until I say I'm no longer interested and I wouldn't count on that happening any time in the foreseeable future."

With that sweet warning filling my ears and heart, I fell asleep in his arms.

Taylor rearranged his schedule so he could spend the next two days with me. I felt as if I were living in a steamy fairytale. We had sex or fucked each morning before taking a shower and a swim. After breakfast, we fucked again with all the eager hunger of two people afraid to admit that we were in danger of falling in love.

We had dinner out each night followed by dancing. When we returned to his house, we spent the night having sex. During those nights when he was sometimes so passionate I felt his heat would consume me. There were also times when his tenderness bought tears to my eyes.

When I cried, he wiped my cheeks and whispered that he never wanted to do anything to make me anything but wildly happy. I was in heaven with him.

Tuesday night when we returned home, he took me out to the pool, and stripped off our clothes.

We lay on towels spread on the grass, kissing and caressing each other until we were both aroused. Then he rose to his knees and urged me to mine. He continued kissing me while he caressed my clit and fingered my pussy. I returned the favor by cupping one hand over his balls and eagerly pumping his cock.

"What's your pleasure tonight?" he asked, sliding his palms over my ass.

I rubbed my cheek against his. "I'm in the mood for some backdoor loving."

He lifted his head to look at me. "Are you sure you're ready for anal sex again?"

"I'm positive."

He kissed me, rose, went inside. When he returned he had a tube of lube and several condoms.

I licked my lips. "Someone's horny," I teased.

"And someone's going to feed me. Isn't she?"

I nodded and got on my hands and knees. "I'm all yours, Taylor."

He bit and kissed my ass until I felt very mellow. Then he spanked me so hard I felt sure I wouldn't be able to sit without discomfort for a week. The thought pleased me.

Then he took me to the pool and drilled my ass with deep, powerful plunges that had me shaking and sobbing uncontrollably within minutes and coming. When he came, he eased out of my sore ass and turned to hug me close as he whispered to me in Tsalagi.

"Yeah well, I think I love you too," I said annoyed that I didn't understand what he was saying.

In response, he lifted my chin and pressed a long, hot kiss against my mouth.

I clung helplessly to him, the emotional and physical desire I felt for him overwhelming me. "Taylor…oh, Taylor."

"It's all right, Shana. I have you. I have you, sweet."

What comforting yet exciting words.

We gathered our clothes and went inside. After sharing a quick shower, we went to bed.

He curled his body against mine and nuzzled my neck.

I fell asleep with him whispering to me in Tsalagi.

In the early morning, I woke to find him between my legs, feasting on my pussy. Damn. Nice. I linked my legs over him and humped his face until I came. Although sated, I prepared to suck him or welcome a fuck. But he slipped behind me and fell asleep.

Oh, hell but a woman could quickly fall in love with such an unselfish lover.

* * *

After breakfast the following morning, he took me back to my hotel since his sons would be spending the night at his house.

"I'm going to miss you tonight, Shana."

"Ditto, Taylor."

He sighed. "You can check out when I pick you up early tomorrow morning before I go to work," he said.

As I lifted my lips for his kiss, I chided myself for how easily I'd fallen in line with whatever plans he made for me. But I knew I would do whatever he wanted me to do.

He lifted his head, breaking the long, heated lip lock we'd shared and blew out a breath. He caressed my cheek. "You are so beautiful and I need and want you more every minute."

I smiled up at him. "You make me burn and feel special when you say things like that."

"You are special." He sighed. "Tonight without you in my bed is going to be the longest night in history." He smiled suddenly and reached down to massage my ass. "The moment we're alone tomorrow, your big, brown ass is mine."

"Don't count your chickens before they're hatched," I said.

He slapped my ass. "Don't tempt me to blow off work and fuck your ass raw now," he said.

I stiffened and shook my head. "You're not fucking my ass without protection."

He arched a brow. "When I said raw, I didn't mean without a condom. I meant until it was sore. I know it's early days, but you're going to need to understand that you're mine to command, Shana. And if I decide I want your ass or your pussy raw, I'll have one or both of them raw."

I sucked in a breath, my heart pounding.

He smiled suddenly. "Don't look so scared, sweet. This sweet obsession we're sharing works both ways."

"Does it, Taylor?"

He nodded and whispered to me in his native tongue.

"Taylor!"

"Yes," he said. "It does. You're mine, but I'm also yours. You can't imagine that I have even a hint of interest in any other woman."

"Can't I?"

"Not unless you're feeling delusional." He bent to kiss my lips. "I'll see you tomorrow, Shana mine."

Shana mine. *Did that make him Taylor mine?* I watched him walk away, fearful that I'd fallen so hard for him that I wasn't sure how long I'd be able to hold out if he were ever reckless enough to insist on fucking me raw.

*  *  *

Alone in my hotel suite, I couldn't stop thinking about him. But I was not going to spend the day mooning over him like a lovesick teenager. While I prepared to spend the day sightseeing, I realized I hadn't called my kids or checked in to make sure everything was running smoothly at the office.

Overcoming a disturbing reluctance to answer possible probing questions from my kids, I called them. Neither picked up so I left messages assuring them that I was fine and having a great time. I then called the office and spoke to my office manager.

Reassured that everything was fine at home and at work, I left the hotel for a day of sightseeing. I visited the Poe House, The Betsy Ross House, took a tour of City Hall and then had a salad at a mall called One Liberty Place. As I sat sipping my diet drink, my cell phone rang.

My heart beat a wild tattoo when my caller I.D. screen read T. Raymond. I lifted the phone to my ear. "Hi," I said.

"Hi, sweet."

His voice was low and warm and I could imagine him smiling that wonderful, sexy smile of his.

"How's your day going?"

"I'm out sightseeing," I said and told him the places I'd already visited and my plans for the rest of the day. "How's your day?"

"Hectic. I've been busy from the moment I left you. I'm pulling up to do an emergency water heater replacement. I have to go. I'll see you tomorrow, sweet."

"Bye," I said.

After lunch, I hopped on a bus and spent a few hours at the Franklin Museum before returning to the hotel during rush hour, which meant I ended up standing all the way back to the hotel on a crowded bus.

Tired from my day out, I undressed, filled the tub, and thankfully sank into the warm scented water. Closing my eyes, I lay thinking of Taylor while I dozed. When I got out of the bath, I decided to spend the night in.

I put on a comfortable, cotton pantsuit and ordered room service.

I was delighted when the room service waiter arrived with a dozen roses, and an expensive box of chocolates from Taylor along with my steak and grilled vegetables.

Smiling, I picked up the card.

*I miss you, Shana mine.*

*Taylor.*

My cell phone rang as I sat watching a movie and thinking about Taylor and how we could make a long distance relationship work. I recognized Jasmin's ring and bit my lip. Then I did something I'd rarely done in our long friendship — ignored her call, allowing it to go to voicemail.

I then spent the rest of the night berating myself for not taking her call. I hadn't because I was afraid she might be calling to tell me she wanted Taylor back. And I didn't want to give him back. I clutched the small teddy bear he'd given me against my breasts.

He found me more natural and had told me about the sons she didn't even know existed. He'd taken time off from work for me. Not her. He hearted me. Not her. And God help me, I hearted him in return.

He called me just after nine. "The guys are popping corn in preparation for a movie we're about to watch. I just wanted to say goodnight."

I smiled. "Oh, Taylor, Taylor. You are too sweet for words."

"Dad!"

He sighed. "Hold that thought. I'll pick you up eight o'clock tomorrow morning after I take the guys to school."

"Good night, Taylor."

"Good night, Shana."

Considering I'd had little sleep since Taylor and I first had sex, I should have slept soundly that night, but I tossed and turned instead. Thoughts of him kept me awake, along with the guilt I felt for blowing off Jasmin's call. Finally, I got up and listened to her message.

"Hey girl, where are you? Give me a call. I've met some amazing men and a satisfying number of them love women just like us—sassy and large. But damn if I haven't found myself comparing every one of them to Taylor. I cannot stop thinking about how wicked he is in bed.

"I hope you're having a good time with him, but not too good because I'm thinking I'm going to be sashaying my ass into his bed when I return. Call me. Love you, girl."

Oh hell! I knew I should call her and confess that things had quickly gotten out of hand with Taylor. But somehow I couldn't.

It took a long time to fall asleep. I woke feeling guilty and tired as hell. But my world brightened tremendously when Taylor arrived, took me in his arms, and kissed me until I couldn't breathe.

I sucked in a deep breath and burrowed in his arms. "Hi."

He laughed, lifted my face, and kissed me again. "Damn. I missed you last night."

"I missed you too."

He sighed, shaking his head. "Shit, this is so intense. I feel like I'm burning every time I think of you and I think of you nearly every waking moment."

The need I heard in his voice matched what I felt. I linked an arm around his neck. "This is crazy, Taylor. We didn't even know each other a week ago and—"

He pressed his fingers against my mouth. "We know, need, and want each other now to the exclusion of everyone else. Yes?"

"Yes," I whispered, pressing my cheek against his shoulder. "Oh lord yes."

"What else matters, Shana mine?"

"I feel like a silly teenager with you and I get such a thrill when you call me Shana mine. And when you do, nothing else matters." *Unless you count a little thing like the lifelong friendship I'll risk if I try to pursue a relationship with you after Friday.*

He smiled. "You are mine and God help anyone trying to take you from me."

"Jasmin called," I said when he released me.

He picked up my suitcase. "Are you ready to checkout?"

"Yes. Jasmin called," I said again, glancing around to make sure I hadn't left anything in the room.

"I heard you the first time, sweet." He opened the suite door and waited for me to walk out in front of him. "And I'm no more interested in what she had to say now than I was yesterday. We had a pleasant but meaningless fling that went on far longer than it should have. End of story and discussion."

For him maybe, but not me—not when I knew I'd be caught between a man I hungered for with a passion beyond reason and my best friend.

We spent a few hours shopping for souvenirs before we went to South Philly to have one of Phillie's famous cheesesteaks for lunch. Then we walked hand in hand along Penn's Landing down by the river.

Each time he stopped to hug or kiss me, I could feel myself falling a little more in love with him.

That night we had dinner while cruising along The Delaware on a dinner cruise ship. He kissed and caressed me at every opportunity and I eagerly responded, all too aware that we were spending our last night together.

We were both quiet on the drive to his house.

"Can you imagine yourself living here?"

Surprised and pleased by the question, I turned to look at Taylor. "What?"

He closed and locked the door and set the alarm before meeting my gaze. "You heard me. Can you?"

I looked around the foyer. I loved the textured floors and the pleasing cream-colored paint. The centerpiece of the foyer was the wide staircase that wound at the top and opened up onto an interior second floor balcony. Each room was tastefully furnished. There were a few things I might change but nothing major.

It seemed like a solid, well-built brick house that had been thoroughly modernized. I shrugged. "It's a very nice house. Who updated and decorated it?"

"I bought it at auction five years ago. It was a wreck and had to be completely gutted."

"That must have been a lot of work."

"It was but I didn't do it alone. I had two mentors. One of them, along with his brothers, and my father helped me completely gut it and rehab it."

"You did a great job."

"One of my mentors is a very skillful carpenter. He took me on as an apprentice and taught me nearly everything I know and encouraged and helped me to start my own business—even sending clients my way he could have kept for himself."

"He sounds like a great guy."

"Both of them are. I'll introduce you to them one day."

"I'll look forward to it. So who decorated it?"

"My mother decorated."

"She has great taste."

He sighed and shook his head. "Now are you going to answer my question?"

"No."

To my surprise, he arched a brow but didn't pressure me for an answer.

After a swim, we undressed and slipped into bed. I was surprised and disappointed when he showed no inclination to make love to me.

He held me all night and woke me early the next morning. "I need you," he whispered, rubbing his erect cock against my thigh.

"Bathroom break," I said.

He reluctantly rolled off me.

When I returned to the bedroom, he sat on one of the chairs by the window with a condom on.

I tossed off the robe I wore and crossed the room to him. Smiling, I placed my hands on his shoulders and rubbed my slit against his cock.

He reached up to squeeze and caress my bare breasts. "Ride me, sweet."

I leaned forward to touch my lips to his forehead. "Which entrance, Taylor?"

"Your sweet pussy."

I sighed in relief and reaching down to part my slit, I pressed it against his cockhead.

Gripping my hips, he pulled them down slowly.

Tightening my hands on his shoulders, I closed my eyes. I enjoyed every second of feeling his hard length pushing up into me until I sat with my ass on his lap savoring the joy of having him buried deep inside me again.

I thought he wanted to fuck, but his gentleness and tenderness as he caressed and kissed me filled with me wonder that I could invoke such deep emotion in him so quickly. When he whispered to me in his native tongue, I lapped up each word—even though I still couldn't understand a word he said.

I sat on his lap with my cheek pressed against his neck after we'd both come. By six that night, I'd be on a plane — leaving him and my heart behind — unless I tossed Jasmin under the bus by starting a long distance relationship with Taylor.

But even if I decided to put desire above friendship, what were the chances he and I would fare any better than he and Jasmin had? Like her, I was nearly ten years older than him. Like her, I lived and worked on the opposite coast from him. Unlike her, I had two kids who would probably think I'd lost my mind thinking I could keep his interest for any extended length of time. And unlike Jasmin, I'd be devastated if he lost interest in me.

I lifted my head to look at him, the muscles of my throat tight. "I'm going to miss you so much, Taylor."

He caressed my back and shoulders. "You won't if you stay here with me until I can accompany you home in a few weeks when I've handled my work commitments. "

That would only make the eventual breakup harder. "I can't."

"Why not?"

I peeled myself off his cock and rose. "I think I'm always going to remember this week with you as the sweetest of my life."

He stood up and caught my hand as I turned away. "But?"

"But I did what I came to do and now it's time for me to go home." *Before I fall hopelessly in love with you.*

"Your kids are nearly adults and living on their own . If you go home without me, what are you going home to?"

I stared at him. "Did it ever occur to you that you just might be overestimating the effect you have on me?"

"No," he said coolly. "That thought never occurred to me. Why should it when we both know it's not true?"

"It's a bit much for you to imagine that unless I have you in my life, it'll be emotionally or romantically empty. We had a fling."

"Oh fuck, Shana. Don't you go there. You know damned well this isn't just a fling for you any more than it is for me."

Staring into his angry gaze, I couldn't deny the truthfulness of his words. "Jasmin probably wants you back," I said.

"I don't want her or anyone but you, Shana."

"She's my best friend."

"And?"

"And I think she wants you back."

"That's too damned bad, isn't it? I told her it was over when we spoke on the phone. But we both know she already knew that."

"That's all well and good for you but what am I supposed to do? Pretend I don't know and won't be betraying her if I ignore how she feels?"

He cupped a hand over my cheek. "Oh, sweet. All she and I shared was sex. We both know there's far more than that going on between us. Yes?"

I nodded. While I knew I did and suspected he felt more as well, I wasn't willing to risk my life-long friendship on the very slim chance that we could build a meaningful relationship despite our various differences.

"Stay."

Saying no to him was nearly impossible but necessary. "You make me feel the world is full of new and exciting possibilities, but if what we think we feel is real—it can withstand a separation. In fact, we're both old enough to know how necessary one is at this point."

He sighed. "Okay. You're right. How do you want to spend the rest of the day?"

"Alone with you."

He smiled. "That's how I'd like to spend the rest of my life."

"Oh, Taylor."

He shrugged. "I'm going to take a quick shower and then I need to fill up my tank. Can I get you anything while I'm out?"

"Just come back as soon as possible."

He kissed me and whispered something against my lips before he turned away.

I snatched at his hand. "What did you say?"

He shook his head. "Nothing you'd be inclined to believe at this point and maybe you shouldn't. Hell, I'm feeling it and I don't know if I believe it."

While he was gone, I showered and carried my suitcase and carry-on shoulder travel bag downstairs. Then I went out to lay in one of the chaise lounges by the pool.

He returned with several sandwiches and a salad.

I nibbled at the sandwich and picked at the salad.

"I'm not hungry either," he said. "Let's go inside and cuddle until it's time to drive you to the airport."

I nodded.

In his living room, we shared his reclining loveseat.

Despite the countless questions I wanted answers to, I lay silent within his arms.

My cell phone rang. I recognized Jasmin's ring. I sighed and then rose to walk across the room to pick up my shoulder bag from the coffee table. I removed my phone and answered it. "Hi."

"Well, it's about time. Didn't you get my message? Where are you?"

I turned to look at Taylor who sat staring at me. "I'm with Taylor."

"Really? Did you have a good time with him?"

"Oh lord yes."

"I don't think I like the sound of that, Shana. I did tell you I wanted him back. Didn't I?"

"Yes and I told him you did."

"And he said?"

"He…ah…" I looked at Taylor and held out the phone. "It's Jasmin."

He rose and quickly crossed the room to take the phone from me. "Jasmin. I was just telling Shana that our causal relationship was over with no hope of a resurrection…trust me. It's over…I'm sorry but I don't share that desire…we were both drunk when that happened…it's over. Here's Shana…how I feel about her is none of your business."

He held the phone out to me. "I don't care what she says, it's over between us, Shana." Walking back across the room, he sat on the loveseat.

I sighed and put the phone back to my ear. "Jasmin?"

"What the hell have you done, Shana? I told you I wanted him back!"

"I know and…I know."

"Have you been staying with him?"

"Yes."

"Where?"

"At his house."

"Oh Shana. How could you? How could you?"

Before I could answer she ended the call.

I closed my eyes and pressed a hand over my mouth. *Oh fuck. What now?*

"Shana?"

I opened my eyes and stared at him. "She thinks I betrayed her."

He rose and extended his hand.

I shook my head. "I need some time alone."

He crossed the room but didn't touch me. "Oh come on, Shana. Don't let this ruin the few remaining hours we have together."

"You can't expect me to go on as if nothing's changed."

He sighed and walked back to the loveseat. "Oh fuck! I wish I'd never met the silly bitch!"

I rushed across the room to stare down at him. "Don't you call her a bitch just because you can't have your way!"

"I called her a bitch because that's what she is! She doesn't want me and I don't want her but damned if she'll allow that little fact to stop her from trying to have her cake and eat it too! Even if she's successful in making you feel so guilty you destroy our relationship, I wouldn't take her back into my life for a million bucks!"

"She's my best friend and she's nothing like you're trying to paint her."

"The hell she isn't."

We were both too angry to continue a conversation I feared would escalate out of control. "Please take me to the airport."

"It's too early."

"I'll wait there."

"If you think I'm prepared to beg, think again. If you're ready to go, I'll drive you to the airport now."

Talk about a rock and a hard place. No matter which choice I made one of them would be hurt and angry. I sighed. "I'm ready now."

He narrowed his gaze. "Shana—"

"Please, Taylor. We had a great week but it's time for me to return to reality."

"Fuck you!" He stormed from the room. I heard the front door open and reluctantly followed him out the house in time to see him putting my luggage into the trunk of his car.

As I approached, he silently held the passenger door open.

I got in and ninety minutes later, I sat alone in the airport, struggling to keep from crying as he stalked away from me.

*Oh, Taylor. Please don't walk away in anger.*

Almost as if he'd sensed my anguish, he suddenly turned and quickly walked back towards me.

My heart raced with joy and hope.

He leaned down to speak to me — in Tsalagi.

I turned my head to meet his angry gaze. "You know I don't know what you're saying, Taylor."

"I said I've never had to beg a woman and I'm not going to start with you. If you're not interested in being my woman, I'll find someone who is. But I can promise you it won't be that manipulative bitch you choose to call a friend!"

"Don't talk about her like that."

He reached in his pocket and pushed a business card in my hand. "If you come to your senses, you know where I live and can reach me at one of these numbers."

"I'm not fond of men who think it's all right to call a woman a bitch!" I looked at the card long enough to memorize his cell phone number and to realize that he was a licensed general contractor before I crushed the card in my hand and threw it at him.

He caught it and jammed it in his pant pocket. "Are you sure you what it to end this way?"

"I'm sure I don't like your tendency to call my best friend a bitch!"

"Fine. Have a good life, Shana."

I sucked in a breath as a tear rolled down my cheek. "Taylor…"

His gaze softened and for one sweet moment, I thought he would draw me into his arms and make everything all right. Instead, he swore, straightened, and walked away.

*Taylor. Oh, Taylor.*

# Chapter six

Tears ran down my cheeks for most of the flight back to San Francisco. I was dismayed to find my son waiting at the airport when I arrived.

I turned away and tried to wipe my cheeks but he must have seen my tears because he rushed forward and put an arm around my shoulders. "Mom! What's wrong?"

I shook my head. "Nothing. I just…nothing."

He got my luggage and led me to his car. After we were seated, he turned to look at me. "Do I need to go to Philadelphia and kick some guy's butt?"

I shook my head. "No. I had an…interlude and I guess I'm a little sad it's over, but I'm fine."

"Are you sure, Mom?"

The one thing I was sure of is that it would take a long time to get over Taylor and I wasn't going to drag my son into my romantic mess. "Yes. I'm sure."

"He didn't hurt you. Did he?"

Physically? No. Emotionally? Big time. I squeezed his hand. "Don't worry, Jimmy."

"You're in tears. How can I not worry, Mom?"

I sighed. "You know I sometimes get emotional. There's no reason for you to worry."

He sighed. "I don't have any plans for tonight. Let's go out to dinner."

I wanted to go home, undress, and then spend hours in a warm bath with a drink — sobbing until I couldn't cry anymore. But I knew Jimmy wanted to feel that he was there for me when I needed someone.

I forced myself to smile. "Who's paying?"

"You are, of course, Mrs. Successful Businesswoman," he said, laughing.

I laughed too. "I should have known."

He took me home for a quick shower and then we headed down to my favorite restaurant at Fisherman's Wharf. Jassy was there when we arrived.

I turned to look at Jimmy.

He shrugged. "I thought you might need us both with you tonight."

Touched, I hugged and kissed them both.

That night with my kids was one of the most special in my life. I teared up a little, laughed a lot, and felt as if I were in a cocoon of love and affection. It was only as I lay in bed sleepless that night that I realized they must have both turned off their phones so I'd have their complete attention.

Hugging that realization close, I fell asleep without tears. The next morning when I turned the ringer on my cellphone back on, I found Jasmin had left several messages. Hurt and angry by our last conversation and her implication that I'd betrayed her, I ignored them.

There were no messages from Taylor. But then I hadn't expected any. I felt certain he was a man of his word and it was over between us — unless I made the first move to change that.

Recalling his unwillingness to bend and his insistence that he had no intentions of making an exception for me, I knew all his hints about falling in love with me had been nothing more than him allowing his cock to do his thinking and talking. If a man wouldn't make an exception for the woman he loved, who would he make them for other than his sons?

While he clearly didn't love me, I knew I'd made the monumental mistake of falling in love with him. Although I ached to be with him, I couldn't see the point of being in a one-sided relationship. It was not going to be easy, but I had to move forward with my life. That meant giving myself a week or two to wallow in regret, and then I'd start dating again.

\* \* \*

Shana Mine

Walking away from Shana was the hardest thing I'd ever done. I left the airport feeling as if I'd been gutted and my heart shredded beyond repair. Telling myself that it was ridiculous to feel such emotions for a woman I'd known for less than a week didn't help.

I'd never been in love before and generally got most of the women I went after. Only Lisa and Jasmin had dumped me. Neither rejection had hurt. Losing Shana definitely hurt like hell.

After two weeks of sleepless nights and picking up the phone to call her nearly every hour, I knew I needed to talk to someone about her. I didn't want to burden my father who had finally reached a point where he'd accepted my mother's death and was ready to start dating again.

I'd spent the last five years building my business and spending as much time with my sons as possible. My friendships had suffered and I'd lost track with most of the men I'd considered friends.

That left the two men who had mentored me, Kristopher Macarik, whose foundation had covered most of the cost of my two years of trade school and Jayven Redwolf, the master carpenter who had taken me under his wing and taught me far more than I'd ever have learned from a trade school alone.

Jayvyn was newly married. While I felt certain he'd make time to listen, he'd probably tell me to fly to San Francisco and insist she return to Philly with me — whether she wanted to or not.

Kristopher was involved in a long-standing and complex relationship that didn't exactly make him an expert on how to land that one special woman. But his advice was less likely to land me in trouble with the law if I followed it than Jayvyn's was.

So I called Kristopher.

"I'm having a weekend bender tonight. Pack an overnight bag and we'll find time to talk during the weekend," he said.

I hadn't been to one of his rowdy, weekend fuck-a-thons in over two years since I'd decided it was time to start setting a better example for my sons. "Thanks, but I'm really not in the partying mood."

"That's just what you need," he countered. "This weekend will be much more mellow. There won't be any naked people running amok over the property and no pool and public sex. Besides, Caine and Joya will be here and he'll probably have more useful advice than I will."

I hadn't seen Kristopher's younger brother Caine since his wedding. But since he had married an older woman who had several kids, I decided Kristopher was right. I needed to talk to Caine. "What time shall I come?"

"Any time you like. I might be a little late but Rayna is there now organizing everything."

Rayna Redwolf was Jayvyn's niece. Like Shana, she was a beautiful, full-figured black woman I'd once had a schoolboy crush on. She'd come to my twenty-first birthday party and engaged me in a slow, hot lip lock that had nearly made me come on the spot. Then she'd slapped my ass and told me I was too young and handsome for her and to go enjoy myself with the ladies.

And I had until I met Jasmin. And then Shana. Shana. Damn. I missed her.

"Still there, Taylor?"

"Yes. I am. Thanks, Macarik. I'll see you tonight."

* * *


My guys were spending Saturday night with me so I only packed an overnight bag and drove to Montgomery County after work where Kristopher had a large modern mansion with an Olympic size and a smaller pool on the grounds of his gated property.

When I arrived, the house was lit and several cars were already in the driveway.

Rayna, looking lovelier than ever, opened the door, took one look at my face, and embraced me.

Feeling encased in the strange warmth and empathy she always projected, I returned her embrace, burying my face against her neck briefly before I pulled away.

She reached out to grip my hands, her dark gaze locking on my face. "It's been ages since we saw each other. How are you, Taylor?"

"I've been better," I admitted.

She nodded, an understanding look in her eyes. "Let's go into Macarik's study and talk."

Even though I'd come to talk to her uncle, I nodded. Underneath the sensual sexiness she projected lay a well of warmth that had always made me feel that no matter what I did, she'd always be willing to offer comfort and a listening, non-judgmental ear.

We went down the hall to his study. She poured us both a drink and we sat on the loveseat. I spoke in Tsalagi since it was also her native tongue. Even before she said a word, I felt better just having her there listening.

"It sounds like she's as in love with you as you are with her but is struggling to keep her friendship intact. You can't really blame her for that, Taylor. When things are darkest, a woman needs her girlfriends more than ever."

"Even if she's a bitch?"

She arched a brow. "Her friend is a bitch because she's still attracted to you?"

I stared at her and then laughed. "No. She's one because she knows it's over between us and she's gone out of her way to ensure Shana and I don't establish a relationship."

"A word of advice, Taylor, stop calling her friend a bitch — even if you thinks she is one. Romantic relationships — no matter how hot and heavy — often fizzle out and die, but a woman's best friend is always her best friend."

"So you think I shouldn't have tried to force her to choose between us?"

"In a word? Yes. Letting her make the choice herself might have been a wiser way to go. Still, you obviously love her and what woman worth the name could resist you?"

I arched a brow. "You never had a problem doing just that."

She laughed and leaned forward to kiss me on the corner of my mouth. "Even if I weren't old enough to be your mother, I've always thought of you almost as a younger relative."

She looked as if she was in her early thirties, but then she'd looked like that since I was a teenager. She, like her three uncles, didn't appear to have aged at all. I'd decided a long time ago not to delve too deeply into how the four of them managed to look as if they were not aging. When I was around them, the word vampire often came to mind. But since I'd seen them all in daylight, that couldn't be the explanation for their slow aging. But who knew if vampires even existed.

She tilted her head and stared at me.

I felt certain she could read my thoughts.

She smiled and opened her mouth, revealing perfectly straight, normal teeth. "I have it on good authority that they do indeed exist, but I'm not one of them. But enough about vamps. What are you going to do about your Shana?"

I sighed, shaking my head. "I don't know."

"Don't you? You love her. She probably loves you. What's not to know?"

I shrugged. "She has a few hang-ups about our age difference and she's always dated black men exclusively."

"So had Jayvyn's wife and maybe Caine's too, but I'm not sure about her. However, I am sure that you shouldn't let her slip through your fingers, Taylor."

I sighed. "I won't, but she's probably right about our needing some time apart."

"Absolutely. You're a young, sexy, Native American hunk at one of Macarik's parties. You should spend the weekend having a last fling pleasing the ladies before you get down to the business of landing your woman."

I frowned. "And if she found out?"

"I wouldn't worry about that. Just be honest about it and if she has any sense, she's doing the same thing. And don't you worry about that either. You both need a couple of romps with other people so there'll be no doubt how you feel when you see each other again."

I frowned. "Why haven't you ever married?"

She sighed. "Because I have three overprotective, intimidating uncles who suffer from the delusion that no man is good enough for me. I've always known that I'd have to get them married before I'd have a chance to enjoy a serious relationship myself."

"Two done and one to go," I said. Two of her uncles had recently married.

"Yes, but Uncle Connor isn't going to be an easy sell." She smiled. "That's why I saved him for last. He's going to make me work hard to settle him."

"You deserve to be happy, Rayna."

"So do you. So fuck your heart out tonight, Taylor." She kissed me on my lips and left me alone in the room to think — of sex. And more sex. After two weeks of abstinence, I was horny as hell.

The next morning I woke up in one of Macarik's guest rooms with a pretty, busty naked woman with smooth dark skin lying beside me. For a moment, I stared at her in surprise. Then I remembered Rayna introducing her to me the night before and our tumbling into bed for a series of quick, hard fucks that had satisfied my physical needs while increasing the ache my heart felt for Shana.

When I started to get out of bed, she woke up and slapped my ass, and we ended up fucking again. And again, despite the physical satisfaction, I felt an emotional emptiness that left me longing for my Shana. Apparently, the days when sex without the emotional and mental high I experienced with Shana would suffice were long gone.

Later, as we ate brunch, I realized I had no idea what her name was. From the wary looks she kept casting my way, I had a feeling she couldn't remember mine either. When I asked if she wanted to go for a drive, she shook her head.

"Thanks, but actually, I'm leaving. It was…nice to meet you," she said and hurried away.

I wondered who she was trying to fuck out of her system as I packed my bag in preparation for going home. Somehow I hadn't gotten a chance to talk to Caine but decided I'd call him on Sunday.

My cell phone rang as I was going out to my car. Recognizing Lisa's ring, I answered. "Hello?"

"Hi, Taylor. Some friends from school are over in Jersey visiting other friends and they'd love to meet the boys and the girls. I know it's late notice, but I was hoping we could switch Saturdays if you didn't have anything special planned."

I didn't like missing my time with my sons but after a few years of bitter spiteful fights, Lisa and I had finally realized being flexible and reasonable was in the best interests of our sons. Now that she was happily married with two little girls, we enjoyed a pleasant relationship. "Sure."

"You can have them for the entire weekend next week to make up for tonight."

"Thanks. Are they there?"

I spoke briefly to them both before I drove home. The house felt empty and I was restless. Keeping my thoughts off Shana proved impossible. After an hour at home alone, I packed another overnight bag and returned to the party.

I was surprised to find Caine lying out by the pool without his wife.

"She and a couple of the other women went riding." He sat up. "Kristopher tells me you need to talk."

I nodded. "Do you have a few moments to talk in private?"

"Sure." He rose. "Grab a beer and we'll use Kristopher's study."

He drank his beer while I told him about my relationship with Shana. "Do you have any regrets?" I asked.

"About marrying her?" He shook his head. "I'm in love with her. She makes me incredibly happy and I couldn't be more thrilled to have her as my wife."

"But you do have some regrets?" I probed.

"As you know, Joya is eleven years older than I am. She has three daughters."

"And?"

He sighed. "When we met they all developed a crush on me, which made life a little difficult. But since they were all in college, I thought it would be no big deal. After a week or two her older daughters got over it, but her youngest daughter...let's just say, she's a pain in the damn ass forever flirting with me and wearing the skimpiest clothes imaginable around me.

"The silly little creature actually thinks she can tempt me away from her mother." He shook his head. "I swear if she wasn't Joya's daughter I'd tell her where the hell she could take her skinny little, flat ass.

"That's the only fly in the ointment of our otherwise happy marriage. Let's hope Shana's daughter doesn't develop a crush on you."

"I'll worry about that if we ever get together again."

"Is there any doubt that you will?"

"I'm not sure," I said. "You and Joya don't have any issues with the age difference?"

"Not anymore. She's the love of my life and she tells me I am hers. With that going for us, why would we allow something as inconsequential as a few years come between us? What more could a man want than I have with her?"

I hesitated before I responded. Caine had no kids and Joya was past the age when she could safely have another child — assuming she even wanted one. "A son?"

He sighed and then slowly nodded. "That would have been nice, but if I had to choose between having a child and Joya, I'd choose her every time.

"You both already have two kids each and aren't interested in having any more. At your stages in life, those nine years won't mean anything — unless either of you make an unnecessary issue of it. Once you're sure she's the one, I don't see a downside for you marrying her."

Caine arched a brow. "We are talking about marriage as your eventual goal. Isn't it?"

I'd never really felt a pressing need to get married. But then I'd never been in love before. I knew Shana wanted to get married again. And I wanted to make her happy. "If I find she's the one, maybe…probably."

"If you have any doubts about that, now's the time to resolve them," he said. "There are a lot of women here who find Native American men mysterious and exciting. As Kristopher would say, make the most of it."

"Is that what you did during the years you and Joya had that long-distance romance?"

Caine shook his head. "No. I pretty much knew the day we met she was the one for me. Of course, I had no idea it would take six damned years to convince her of the same thing, but I did. She's everything I ever wanted in a woman, lover, and wife.

"If you find you feel that way about Shana, don't sweat the small stuff that will work itself out. And don't hesitate and risk letting her get away. Trust me, Taylor, there's nothing that compares to being married to a woman who loves you as deeply as you do her. Nothing."

"You've given me a lot to think about. Thanks."

He nodded and we went back out to the pool.

The ladies' had returned from their ride and the look of joy I saw on Joya's face when she saw Caine made me long to see the same look on Shana's face. But I still wasn't ready to admit that equated to love.

That evening I spent the night with a different woman — with the same result as I'd had the night before. The physical satisfaction alone wasn't enough anymore. I left Kristopher's house with the conviction that I'd give it a few more weeks and then it would probably be time to talk to my father and my sons about Shana.

\* \* \*

During the weeks after my return to San Francisco, my job, my kids, and my friends kept me too busy for the next two weeks to have much time to brood over Taylor. And even though I thought of him often, once I was alone and ready for bed, I was generally too tired to do anything other than fall asleep.

At the beginning of the third week, Jasmin returned. I found her waiting for me when I returned home after a late dinner with one of our mutual friends.

"I'm so sorry, Shana," she said before I could decide if I even wanted to speak to her. "I need you to talk to me. I can't stand this…division between us. I know it's my fault and I'm here to make amends, if you'll let me."

Her eyes glistened with tears and she looked almost as unhappy as I felt.

I was still pissed but damn if I would lose Taylor and her. I nodded.

We made tea, kicked off our shoes, and sat in my living room staring at each other in silence.

"You really liked him?" she finally asked.

"Liked? No." I shook my head. "Love? Yes."

"You loved him?" She bit her lip and gripped her hands. "I know he's good in bed, but—"

"Just because it was all about the size of his cock for you doesn't mean that's all it was for me too!"

"Shana—"

"No! You listen for a change. It was far more than that for me…for us. I felt an emotional connection with him that I haven't really felt with anyone else, but don't you worry, Jasmin. When you decided you wanted him back, he pushed me to choose between the two of you and like a fool, I chose you."

She made a small sound of distress. "And now you're sorry?"

I bit back the instinctive urge to shout yes. She and I had shared all of the good and bad times in each other's lives. I couldn't imagine my life without her as my best friend. "I'm sorry you forced me to choose between you two—especially when we both know you never really wanted him."

"I didn't know you felt so strongly about him, Shana."

I shrugged. "It doesn't matter now because it's over."

Tears ran down her cheek as she rose and crossed the room to kneel at my feet. "Oh, girl. I'm so sorry. I never meant to do anything to hurt you. I'll make it right with him."

I shook my head. "There's nothing to make right. I love him and I think he has an affection for me, but he doesn't love me."

"Are you sure, Shana?"

I nodded and kneeled besides her, allowing the tears I'd been holding back to run down my cheeks. "If he felt any more than affection for me, he wouldn't have just let me walk away from him. Or he would at least have followed me or made some effort to contact me."

"Can you tell me about your week with him?"

Finally. Someone I could talk to about him and the hole the end of our brief relationship had left in my heart.

We rose and shared the loveseat and I told her about my interlude with Taylor.

"You're probably giving up on him too soon. It's only been a little over two weeks and — "

"That's more than enough time, Jasmin. All the real feelings were on my side."

"How can you say that? I knew him much longer than you did and stayed in Philly for two weeks on three separate occasions while we were dating. Yet, I was never invited to his house and I didn't even know he had sons. And I couldn't get him to take a single damned day off from work when I visited. I had to amuse myself during the day while he worked. Now I know why he was never free on Wednesday nights and every other Saturday night.

"I think it's safe to say he's already made exceptions for you. Give him time to make the ultimate one and please forgive me, girl. You are the last person I'd ever want to hurt. You know that. Don't you?"

We'd been through too much to doubt that. Yet, I was still a little pissed but I was unwilling to give up the friendship that had meant so much to me over the years. I nodded.

She compressed her lips and shook her head. "I think you should know that he was more than a little interested in you before you two met. I showed him your picture and I think part of me knew then, it was game over for us. He got this far away look in his eyes and was forever asking questions about you after that.

"When he talked about coming for a visit, I dissuaded him. You know why? Because I think I knew in my heart that he'd be coming to meet you and not see me. I owe you such an apology. I should not have stepped between you two when I knew what would probably happen when you two met. It would have been clear to an idiot that he'd already fallen for you.

"Once he saw your picture, the heat level in our relationship went from 120 degrees down to about 10. Looking back, he probably only continued it so he could pick my brain about you."

I stared at her, shocked and hurt by her confession and the realization she had knowingly tried to derail our budding relationship. "Why?"

She sighed. "Because it wasn't just sex for me with him. I fell for him too, Shana but after he saw your picture, he wanted you. I know this sounds bad and it is, but please forgive me. Yes, I tried to come between you too, but I also brought you two together."

"And tore us apart, Jasmin! Why? Are you in love with him too?"

"No. I liked him…hell, I still like him a lot, but it hasn't escalated to love."

"Damn Jasmin! If you were in love with him too, I could understand your behavior. But you forced me to choose between you and him for no real reason. I've lost the man I love because you couldn't accept the fact that he preferred me to you."

She bit her lip, shaking her head. "I have no excuse for what I did. I don't know why I did it, but I am so sorry. Forgive me?"

I shook my head. "Right now I think we need some space and I need to evaluate our friendship."

"Shana—"

"No, Jasmin. I need to get to a place again where I don't feel as if my feelings are so inconsequential to you that you'd find doing something like that acceptable."

"Oh, girl, please. I'm so sorry."

I took a deep breath and looked away from her tears. "Just give me a few weeks to deal with everything and then we'll talk again."

"I got a little crazy because he's so good in bed, but —"

"I really don't want to hear how good you think he is in bed, Jasmin. I don't want to hear anything about either one of you. He's out of my life for good and I want you out of it for the next few weeks.

"Just leave me alone to deal with things and we'll talk in a few weeks and figure out how to get our friendship back on track."

She nodded and left in tears. Alone, I got in bed and spent most of the night crying for the ache for Taylor that seemed to grow more intense with each passing day and for the damage my friendship with Jasmin had suffered. If I'd had any real hope that Taylor might one day fall in love with me, I would gladly have tossed my pride aside and rushed back to Philadelphia and into his arms.

I spent the next two weeks writing and managed to finish my first full-length romance. To celebrate, I had dinner with my kids and went to a swinger's weekend retreat with Jasmin. We solidified our friendship and each had two one-night stands.

Both the men I slept with were adequate in bed and kept me occupied and sexed up for the weekend. But I returned home more in love with Taylor than ever.

I spent a few days in the office. During slow periods of the day, I managed to find a freelance editor with the experience to edit my book. After a little haggling, we agreed on a price and I sent my book to her to for editing. When she finished the edits, I planned to self-publish it.

Feeling restless and lonely, I started on a sequel to the book I'd finished. However, I couldn't concentrate on writing fictional love scenes when I longed to create real ones with Taylor.

# Chapter Seven

Five weeks after I'd last seen Shana and had spent two separate weekends trying to fuck her out of my system with various women, I was finally ready to admit that was not going to happen. What I felt for her was real. And it was time to do something about it.

I had a major project I needed to handle first that would require me to be onsite to supervise for several weeks. I discussed the possibility of withdrawing my bid with Kristopher.

"Don't do that," he said. "You don't want to develop a reputation as a contractor who takes on more than he can handle."

"I know, but I don't think I want to leave her hanging much longer. I can call her but since I was a dumbass and told her I wouldn't make any exceptions for her, I need to get my ass in gear and go see her in person."

"Fine, but don't withdraw your bid yet. Let me talk to Jayvyn to see what we can come up with. But it's time you train someone you can trust to oversee such projects so you don't find yourself in this position again."

Having him point out the obvious made me feel as if he were taking me to task as he'd done when I was young and dumb. But I couldn't take issue with the truth so I held my tongue.

An hour later, Jayvyn called and told me he'd oversee the project for me until I returned from San Francisco.

"Thanks," I said, feeling as if a weight had been lifted from my shoulders.

"Go take care of business and leave the job to me."

"How do you want to handle your fee?" I asked.

"I didn't ask for a fee."

"Thanks, Jayvyn, but I'd have to pay anyone else."

"I'm not anyone else. I'm the man who spent more than two years mentoring you. I have a vested interest in your continued success. I don't need or want a fee. You can thank me by bringing her to meet us when you've sealed the deal and by mentoring in your turn."

I owed both him and Kristopher a lot. After I'd graduated from trade school, I'd spent five years working for Jayvyn before he and Kristopher had financed the start of my own company. "I will," I promised.

After I hung up, I went on line to check flights to San Francisco and then called my father and my sons' mother, Lisa. Although I was nervous at the step I was about to take, I was also excited at the thought of seeing Shana again and telling her how I felt.

* * *

Six weeks after leaving Philadelphia, I woke one morning and knew I was going to be miserable until I at least saw Taylor once more and tried to start a real relationship with him.

I talked to my kids and made a reservation to fly to Philly on Friday. With my decision made, I experienced a certain level of relief. Although I had no idea what kind of reception I could expect from Taylor, I felt better knowing I was finally going to try to win back his interest.

With three days left before I'd see him again stretching before me, I couldn't sleep. I wanted to call him, but was afraid of his reaction. I hoped that seeing me in person would make it harder for him to walk away from me again. My fully edited book had been collecting dust on my hard drive because I was afraid of bad reviews.

Since I was taking the plunge with Taylor, I decided it was time to go all the way in every aspect of my life. I formatted my book, said a prayer, and submitted it to several online sites. And waited and waited for someone—anyone to buy my book.

Two days later, I'd only sold a few copies. Clearly, I would not be quitting my day job anytime soon.

On Wednesday night, after a hard day at work, during which nothing went right, I drove to the airport to meet Jasmin who was returning from a trip to Chicago. A flight from Philadelphia was announced and I sighed as my thoughts turned towards Taylor. What I wouldn't give to be there to meet him.

*Get a grip, Taylor. You'll see him in two days.* Tearing my thoughts away from him, I waited impatiently, my thoughts on a few drinks, a long soak, and hopefully a night of undisturbed sleep.

"Hey, girl."

I looked up in surprise as Jasmin walked towards me from the direction of airport entrance. "Where's your luggage?" I asked, rising and wondering why and when she'd walked passed me without my seeing her.

She sighed. "I have a confession."

"What?" I asked, walking towards the entrance. "Where's your luggage?"

"You're not here to meet me, Shana."

"What?" I stared at her, annoyed. "I've had a lousy day and I am not in the mood for any shit from you, Jasmin. Why am I here?"

"Hopefully to welcome us to San Francisco."

The deep, warm voice sent a thrill of delight through me. My heart raced as I swung around.

Taylor stood behind me.

"Oh, my God. Taylor!" I rushed to him.

He engulfed me in a warm embrace.

Within the circle of his arms, I felt his warm lips against my ear. He whispered something in his native tongue. Of course, I didn't understand a word, but the passion and intensity I heard in his voice filled me with hope. I clung to him. Then I frowned. "Us?"

"Us." He kissed my neck. "My father and the guys are with me."

I pulled away from him.

He put an arm around my shoulders and turned me around.

For the first time I noticed three males standing to one side watching us. I recognized all three of them. The oldest was obviously Taylor's father. The two younger males were his sons.

My eyes filled with tears and I bit my lip in an effort to control the emotions raging through me. His bringing his sons sealed the deal for me. There was no way he would introduce them to me unless he was as seriously interested in me as I was in him.

He walked me over to them. "Dad, this is Shana Morgan. Shana, this is my father, Taylor Raymond."

He took my hand between both of his and smiled. "It's a pleasure to meet you, Ms. Morgan."

What a thrill to have an idea of how handsome and sexy Taylor would still be in twenty-five years. "It's very nice to meet you, Mr. Raymond."

Taylor motioned to his sons. The tallest one, who appeared to be an inch or two taller the other three males, stepped forward with his hand extended.

"Shana, this is Taylor Raymond Donovan. We call him, J.R. J.R this is Shana, Morgan."

"Hi," he said in a voice almost as deep as his father's.

I smiled, giving him my hand. "I'm so happy to meet you."

"And this is Raymond Taylor Donovan," Taylor said of his other son who was an inch or two shorter than his father. "Ray, this is Shana Morgan."

Taylor's youngest son smiled. "She's pretty, Dad."

Taylor looked at me and smiled. "Yes she is."

"Thank you, Ray." I looked up at Taylor, blinking rapidly to keep my gaze tear-free. "Where are you heading?"

"To see you. My father and the guys are getting back on a plane and heading to Florida where the guys are vacationing with their mother, stepfather, and little sisters. Dad came with them so they could all meet you." He looked at Jasmin. "Thanks for getting her here."

Jasmin flashed him a quick smile before she leaned close to kiss my cheek. "Don't let him get away this time," she said, winked at me, and walked away.

He looked at me.

Meeting his gaze, I felt a thrill of anticipation at the thought of spending the night in his arms again. I forced my thoughts away from sex. "What do we have time for?"

"We have three hours before they're flying back out. We want to spend it with you."

We sat in the airport lounge talking until it was time for the others to board their plane. At least they talked and I spent most of my time trying not to stare at Taylor and keep my hands off him.

Watching Taylor's father embrace him and kiss his cheek and seeing him repeat the show of affection with his sons, drove home how close all four must be.

"They are so handsome," I said when we were in my car driving away from the airport.

"They take after my father," he said.

I cast a quick glance at him. "So do you. When do I get to meet your mother?" I asked nervously.

"My mother died three years ago."

"Oh. I'm so sorry."

"Thanks. We all still miss her. And when do I get to meet your parents?"

My parents had retired to Georgia when the kids started college. I had a feeling Mom would think Taylor was handsome but Dad would not be pleased that he wasn't black. "Whenever you feel like winging your way to Atlanta."

"We'll have to make arrangements."

And I'd have to warn Mom so she could work on Dad who would otherwise give Taylor a very chilly reception. "Okay. Is your father dating?"

"Not yet but I think he's finally ready to entertain the idea."

"I'm sure the women will be beating a path to his door when he is."

"No doubt about that, but I'm not particularly interested in discussing anyone's love life but my own."

"Okay, Mr. It's-all-about-me."

He laughed.

Lord I loved the sound of his laughter. "Where are you staying?"

"With you. Where else?"

"How long do I have you?"

"A week. Then my father and I will fly down to Florida to get the guys. We're going to spend a week camping."

I glanced at him. "So I have a week to make you mine?"

He shook his head. "I've been yours the moment we met. Nothing's happened in the last seven weeks to change that."

His wording reminded me of how I'd spent the last week—with other men trying to forget him. Something in his tone told me he'd probably done the same thing. But I didn't care because at that point I was convinced his heart was mine for the taking.

We made a stop at my favorite Chinese restaurant for takeout, bought a bottle of wine, and went to my apartment.

The moment we closed the entrance door of my apartment, he dropped his bags, and leaned back against the door to smile at me.

My heart racing, I put the wine and the food on the hall table. Then, moistening my lips, I kicked off my heels, peeled off my hose, and then slowly removed my dress. Placing it over the chair at the right side of the small table there, I stood facing him in my bra and thong.

He stared at me in silence as he removed his clothes. Deliciously naked, he leaned back against the door, his erect shaft protruding in front of his big, buff body. He offered me a condom.

"I want to taste you."

He smiled. "So who's stopping you, sweet?"

I took the condom and dropped to my knees in front of him. Allowing the small package to slip from my fingers, I gripped his hips and leaned forward to twirl my tongue around the tip of his cock. Encountering the pre-cum seeping from it, I lapped it up with my tongue, and slid my mouth forward.

I enjoyed the feel and taste of his flesh on my lips and against my tongue. I sucked him slowly.

He inhaled sharply. "Oh...sweet."

As before, he allowed me to set the pace.

I sucked him with a slow, steady pressure while reaching a hand down to cup and massage his balls. They were round and heavy and I longed to feel their contents spill into my mouth and on my lips as he came.

He cupped his hands over my head, inching his hips forward. "Shit! I'm about to come...unless you want a mouthful, now's the time to pull out."

I released his balls and gripped his ass cheeks. Digging my fingers in, I sucked him harder and deeper.

He groaned, curled his fingers in my hair, and exploded inside my mouth.

I drew back slowly until the tip of his cock rested against my mouth. I licked my lips and rose to kiss him.

He engulfed me in his arms, with his lips against my ear. "Shana, oh my beautiful Shana, I can't tell you how much I've missed you…the nights I spent dreaming about holding you like this again."

I burrowed closer into his arms. "Jasmin called you?"

"Yes, but I was coming any way."

"When? When it was too late because I'd found someone else?"

He stepped back and stared down at me. "Don't kid yourself. Your chances of finding a man capable of making you forget me were no better than mine of finding a woman to take your place in my arms, bed, or heart."

"But you tried?"

He nodded. "That's how I knew there was no getting over you."

I sighed, sliding my hands over his bare chest. "I found that out too — after I tried."

"And now we know we belong together. Yes?"

I nodded. "Yes. Oh yes, Taylor."

"Good. Now we've got that out of the way, I'm starving."

I stared at him. "What?"

He took my hand in his. "Let's eat."

"In case you haven't noticed we're both naked."

He locked his gaze briefly on my breasts and pussy before smiling at me. "Oh believe me, I've noticed. But I'm still starving. If you expect me to spend the night fucking the hell out of you, you're going to have to feed me first."

I experienced a jolt of need at his words. "Then why are we standing around talking? The food is getting cold." I picked up the bottle of wine and take-out and walked into the living room.

"I'll get glasses and some plates," I said, nodding towards the loveseat. "You keep that warm."

He sat with his legs parted, his semi-erect shaft lying along one of his muscular thighs. "I'll be waiting," he said.

When I returned, we turned down the lights, and ate by candlelight. "Why did you let me go, Taylor?"

He kissed my shoulder. "I didn't want to but you were right. We needed some time apart. We had it. We had other lovers and we still want each other to the exclusion of everyone else. Yes?"

I nodded. "Oh yes, and yes again."

"Good. Now. When do I get to meet your kids?"

I bit my lip. "Strangely enough, both of them are in Florida at the moment."

He trailed s finger down my neck to my breasts. "For how long?"

"For another ten days or so."

He pinched my right nipple. "Can you fly down with me when I go pick up my guys so you can introduce us?"

"Well…yes."

Still pinching my nipple, he turned my face to his with his other hand. "But? Are you trying to tell me you don't want us to meet?"

"No. It's not that…" I sighed. "You'll have to grow on them."

"Why? What did you tell them about me?"

"I was in tears when I returned home. My son surprised me by meeting me at the airport. He called his sister and they put me in a cocoon of affection for several weeks. I never said anything bad about you but my kids are very protective of me and not overly fond of anyone who makes me cry."

He sighed. "I see. Well I can hardly fault them for being upset with anyone who drives you to tears. I still want to meet them."

"Okay."

He kissed my neck and massaged my breasts. "And now I need some pussy. You have any idea where I can get some?"

"Nope. Sorry." I pushed his arm and hand away and stood up. Before I could take a step away, he slapped my ass cheeks and pulled me back on the loveseat and into his embrace.

I put my arms around him and kissed him. The words *I love you* trembled on my lips. I held them back, uncertain if he was ready to hear them yet.

He lay back on the loveseat, pulling me on top of him. "Shana."

The passion and need he imbued in my name touched me. I stared down at him, recalling how bleak my life had felt without him. "Taylor…oh Taylor. I'm so happy to be with you again."

"The feeling is mutual, my beautiful Shana."

I reached behind him to loosen the tie on his hair. I spread the long, dark tresses across his broad shoulders. "Take what's yours, Taylor. My pussy, my ass, my mouth. Everything I have is yours for the taking."

Placing a hand on the back of my neck, he drew my head down to his until our lips touched.

I sighed and closed my eyes.

He kissed me slowly and deeply, stroking his hands down my body to cup over my ass.

Feeling his cock pressed between our bodies made me hungrier for him. Placing my hands on his shoulders, I dragged my mouth away from his and rubbed my pussy against his cock. "Oh God, Taylor. It's been so long." I wrapped my fingers around his shaft. "Fuck me."

"It's going to be just a little longer," he whispered, drawing my lips back down to his.

I loved feeling his big, warm, calloused hands caressing and massaging my body and setting it on fire as no other man had. My nipples hardened and my pussy flooded. I moaned against his lips as I rubbed my breasts against his chest.

With each kiss and caress, my need for him grew along with the urge to whisper that I loved him.

I tore my mouth from his. "Fuck me. Please."

He maneuvered me onto my back and buried his face between my breasts.

"Oh yes, love. Yes."

He kissed a path down over my belly to my pussy.

"No. No." I gripped his shoulders. "It's been too long. I don't want you to eat me. I want you to fuck me. Please."

He lifted his head and rose.

"Where are you going?" I asked.

"Condom," he said.

I frowned, what had happened to the one he'd given me earlier?

He crossed the room to his clothes and pulled out his wallet. He rolled the condom over his cock as he returned to the loveseat. He leaned down to brush his lips against my ear and neck. "Do you want me?"

"Yes. Oh lord yes,"" I moaned, parting my legs and pushing my hips off the loveseat.

He smiled. "Somebody's a little on the horny side — just when I've decided I'm not in the mood."

"Fuck your mood." I wrapped my fingers around him. "Don't make me take this."

He laughed. "I love a woman who knows what she wants." He positioned himself between my thighs and pushed his hips forward.

I gasped and gripped his arms as he slowly pushed his cock deep into my pussy.

"Is this what you want, sweet?" he asked.

I nodded. "Oh…God…yes…yes!" I closed my eyes and licked my lips. "Fuck me."

"Open your eyes and look at me."

I obeyed but jerked at his arms, trying to pull him down on top of me.

Smiling, he moved his hips back and forward, sliding in and out of me with a deliberate passion and heat that surged through every inch of my body. I was on fire for him and filled with an emotion stronger than I'd felt with my ex.

Sex with him was so intense because he stirred me as no other man had. With him inside me, the most powerful emotions of my life assailed me. I curled my fingers in his hair and sobbed as I came. "I love you…I love you…I love you."

He clutched me close and fucked me so hard my thighs shook with each thrust and I arched into him and came again.

As I did, I was only vaguely aware of him whispering to me as he came. I pulled his weight down on me and wrapped my arms and legs around him. "Lord I love you."

He kissed my neck and sighed. "Are you sure?"

"Yes. I'm sure."

He lifted his head to stare down at me. "Shana mine…finally."

Hearing that endearment I had given up on hearing again brought tears to my eyes. I shook my head. "I've been yours for the taking from the moment we met."

He sat on the loveseat and urged me onto his lap. He whispered against my ear.

I pushed him away. "I will learn to speak Tsalagi, but for now I need a translation."

He caressed my cheek. "I've been smitten from the moment I saw your picture. By the time we met, I was and am in love with you. I love you and I want to marry you."

I sucked in a breath and stared at him with happy tears streaming down my cheeks. I wasn't sure how his sons would feel about having me as a step-mom but I knew my kids weren't going to be thrilled to have a stepfather only nine years their senior. One of us would have to relocate since I had no interest in a long-distance relationship.

We'd have challenges—just as every couple did. Challenges or not, I loved him and I wanted him. I was going to have him.

"Will you marry me?"

I nodded. "Hell yeah."

He hugged me close. "I love you, Shana mine."

"I am yours. All yours."

* * *

I lay awake long after Shana had fallen asleep in my arms trying to decide the best way of asking her to relocate to Philadelphia without making her think I thought it was more important I stay near my sons than she did her kids.

I really couldn't afford to lose the job Jayvyn was overseeing for me nor did I have the ability to start all over again on the West Coast. If she didn't want to move, our only alternative would be to have a long-distance relationship, which held little appeal. But having admitted how I felt, I couldn't give her up. Nor could I move across country and leave my guys' stepfather to guide them into young adulthood. He was a decent man and treated them well. But it was my job to help make my guys good men and I wasn't going to cede that responsibility to anyone else.

I fell asleep determined to tackle the subject after breakfast the next day. I never got the chance because I woke the next morning to find a gloriously naked Shana straddling my hips and rolling a condom over my cock.

"Good morning, handsome."

I smiled and reached up to massage her breasts. "Damn. What a great way to start the day."

She caressed my cheeks. "Did you know you talk in your sleep?"

I shook my head. Damn. No one had ever told me that. "I hope I didn't say anything I shouldn't have."

"So you're worried that you whispered another woman's name?"

I stiffened. "What? Shana, I—"

She pressed her fingers against my lips, smiling. "You don't have to worry, Taylor. Your sleep talk was about your kids and not being able to leave them."

"Damn. I—"

"It's all right, Taylor. Your kids are younger and mine will soon be twenty-one. They're both already both living away from home. I'll make the move."

I sucked in a deep, relieved breath. "Oh, sweet. Are you sure?"

"I'm sure I don't want to live away from you and I understand you wanting to be there for your guys while they're still so young. I think living on the East Coast will take some getting used to, but I love you and it's a sacrifice I'm willing to make for you, Taylor mine."

Taylor mine? I could probably hear the endearment several times a day for the rest of my life without it ever losing its thrill, I thought as she lifted her hips and slowly slid the sweetest, warmest pussy in the world down on my clock. Taylor hers? Oh hell yeah. Forever.

# Loving Large — Yours, Only And Always Excerpt

By Marilyn Lee

Published by Marilyn Lee Unleashed

"Don't despair. When you least expect it, the hurt from Sam will dissolve and you'll fall head over heels in love again. It could happen at any time in any place. Just make sure you're ready to accept and embrace it when it happens."

Autumn Walker's mother's words flashed into her mind the moment she walked into the condo association meeting and saw him.

The man who caught her attention was tall, with long legs, wide shoulders, a narrow waist, and a taut ass. He might have stepped right off the cover of one of the Native American capture romances she and her friends had devoured as teenagers. She could easily imagine him bare-chested with long, very dark, silky hair pulled back from his face and hanging down his back as he sat astride a horse without a saddle.

Two women, who she suspected were more interested in spending time in his bed than they were in discussing proposed changes in condo fees, commanded his attention.

She stared at him, feeling herself going wet. What woman wouldn't want to be up close and personal with a man who was so sexy just the sight of him generated capture fantasies?

What she wouldn't give for the courage to strut across the room and join the two women clambering for his attention. She sighed. If only she were tall and slender with mounds of flowing locks like the women vying to hold his interest. But the handsome, sexy male who looked as if he'd just finished posing for the cover of a romance novel wasn't likely to be impressed with her five-foot, five-inch plump body or her dark brown skin. He probably preferred the tall, slender, blue-eyed blondes gazing so adoringly up at him.

Almost as if he felt her eyes on him, he suddenly turned his head, glanced briefly in Autumn's direction, looked away, and then did a double take. He arched a brow and locked his gaze with hers.

Embarrassed at having been caught staring, Autumn still couldn't look away from his dark, sexy, probing gaze. Her heart raced and the erotic imagination she'd struggled to control since her divorce quickly flooded her mind with visions of standing naked before him while he ran his big hands all over her body. Her cheeks burned at the delicious thought of feeling his smooth palms spanking her naked, dark ass cheeks until they burned with heat.

Oh to feel him lubing her up before he gripped her hips and fucked her ass, slow and deep. She bit her lip, going wet as she mentally savored the thought of him cupping his hands over her breasts as he thrust in and out of her rear.

She wore a pretty pink dress with a skirt that ended just below her knees. He could easily push it up to expose a hot pink thong. Once he pushed that skimpy piece of fluff aside he'd have easy access to both her ass and her pussy.

He arched a brow while the corners of his sensual lips slowly curved upward into an appreciative smile. His gaze shifted down to her breasts for several long moments before he looked into her eyes again.

Autumn caught her breath. Was she imaging things or did she detect a hint of interest in his gaze? He had definitely checked out her breasts.

Both blondes glanced at Autumn. One then touched his arm. The other placed a hand against his chest.

I guess they're telling you he's off limits. As if you need that warning.

The object of all three women's desire turned his attention back to the women at his side.

Autumn released a sigh of disappointment, still unable to tear her gaze away from him. He was so sexy.

He spoke briefly to the two women before turning his attention back to Autumn.

She swallowed and stared into his almost hypnotic eyes. He must be interested in her.

The women spoke to him again, seemingly determined to reclaim his attention.

Briefly turning his gaze back to the women, he flashed a smile and spoke to them.

Autumn watched in amazement as he then quickly strolled towards her, ignoring the women's efforts to keep him at their sides.

She swallowed and moistened her lips while her heart hammered against her ribcage.

He stopped a foot or so in front of her. He extended his hand. "Hello." He had a deep, sexy voice.

"Hi."

"I'm Seneka Elkhorn."

Seneka Elkhorn. Nice name. Nice voice. Nice body. Sexy as hell man.

She held out her hand.

A shiver of anticipation danced down her spine when his fingers closed over hers. She imagined him whispering sweet nothings in her ear in that deep, velvety voice as he caressed her bare skin with the big warm hand cradling hers.

"And you are?"

She blinked. "I'm sorry. What?"

"What's your name? Mine's Seneka Elkhorn."

Get a grip, woman and stop gawking as if you've never met a drop-dead gorgeous hunk. "Autumn Walker."

His eyes lingered on her bare left hand. "Autumn is my favorite time of the year."

"Oh…is it?"

"Oh yes." He smiled. "I see you're not wearing a ring, but is there a Mr. 'She's All Mine So Back Off' lurking somewhere?"

She'd never been happier to be divorced and commitment free. She shook her head. "Not anymore."

His smile widened. "No? This must be my lucky night."

His lucky night? Lost in a haze of erotic fantasies, she racked her brain for some witty remark that would titillate and entertain him while making him want to get to know her.

She stole a glance at his left hand. Bare. Thank God.

The association president went to the podium. "Good evening, everyone. We have a number of issues on the agenda so please find seats so we can begin."

Autumn stifled a groan. Why did the blasted meeting have to start on time? She reluctantly withdrew her hand from his. "I guess I'd better find a seat."

He slipped a hand under her elbow. "Yes. Let's do that."

His fingers on her bare skin sent a tingle through her. She turned back to face him, hoping she'd managed to conceal her emotional turmoil from him. "I see a seat —"

"A seat?" He nodded toward two empty seats on the other side of the room. "There are two over there. Join me?"

She hesitated. Contemplating flirting with him as they waited for the meeting to start was one thing. Sitting with him might be too close to a line she'd never crossed before. Her divorce from Sam still stung. The reason he'd divorced her hadn't changed enough to make a difference in her life.

"Autumn," his fingers tightened on her elbow. He leaned down until his lips were a breath away from her ear. "I won't hurt you," he promised softly.

She stared up into his dark eyes. Why did she feel as if he'd read her mind and knew of her hurt? "What?"

"You can trust me, Autumn."

Trust didn't come easy. Sam had broken her heart, injured her pride, and damaged her self-esteem. When Sam left her, she'd decided lost love hurt and that love in general was overrated. Since then she had managed to remain romantically unscathed by channeling all her time and energy into preparing her students for careers in math and science.

Some of her students had done very well. She found satisfaction in celebrating their triumphs with them. Her life wasn't exciting. It was safe. Safety was important.

He caressed her elbow. "You can trust me, Autumn."

Her desire to accept his word and trust him gave her pause. She knew nothing about him except that she found him more sexually exciting than any man she'd ever met. He seemed to want to spend at least an hour or so in her company. An hour wouldn't make much difference to him but it might act as a balm to her wounded ego.

She smiled up at him. "Okay."

"Great." He gave her a slow, warm smile before he led her over to the two empty chairs on the other side of the room. Once she was seated he sat so close to her, his thigh pressed against hers.

She attempted to draw her thigh away from his.

He responded by shifting in his seat in a manner that allowed him to press his thigh against hers again.

She inhaled sharply and glanced at him.

He arched a brow and ensured she was even more aware of him by sliding an arm along the back of her chair. He leaned so close she felt his breath on her cheek. "Relax, Autumn. I don't bite — at least not in public."

She blushed and turned her attention back to the front of the room. If he touched her, she wasn't sure how she'd respond.

He didn't.

Nevertheless, she spent the entire meeting wondering if he were as aware of her as she was of him. His thigh pressing against hers seemed to indicate he was yet each time she stole a glance at him, his attention was on the podium. Later, she couldn't remember how she'd voted on the proposed condo fees.

After the meeting ended, he turned to look at her. "So you're all for increased condo fees?"

"What makes you think that?"

He shrugged. "You raised your hand when the president asked for a show of hands of those in favor of the higher fees."

"I did?"

His lips twitched. "You did."

"Oh…hell!"

He laughed. "It would probably have passed anyway. Now for a really important question, do you have any plans for the rest of the night?"

"No.

"Will you have a drink with me?"

The thought that she might somehow parlay the drink invitation into a night of wanton and uncommitted sex, excited her senses and helped relax her inhibitions. "I'd like that," she admitted.

"So would I." He smiled.

He smiled a lot and lord what a warm, intimate smile. He was so handsome it was difficult not to stare at him.

"Are you ready, Autumn?"

After three years of celibacy she was more than ready to subject herself to any situation that would increase the possibility of their ending up in bed for the night. As improbable as she'd thought it before the meeting started, she was now convinced he shared her sexual interest.

She nodded. "Yes, I'm ready."

Loving Large: Yours, Only And Always is available from Marilyn Lee Unleashed

# Soul Mates Excerpt

## Prologue

"Trey! Trey, help me! Please!"

Her screams for him shattered the still of the night and sent Trey Brandauer bolting up in bed from a deep sleep. He tossed the bed covers aside, nearly tripping in his haste to get out of bed and rush to the window.

His room overlooked the back road leading to the slave quarters. Looking out the window, he saw his father's overseer, Joshua Wilton astride his big stallion. A small slender figure sat in front of him on the horse with her face turned up towards the house.

Trey's heart thumped with fear as he recognized the female's beautiful dark skin. The sweet smile he'd never been able to resist was missing. Her brown eyes held a look of fear.

"Carlee!"

When she saw him, she reached out with a trembling hand. "Trey! Please help me!"

Trey tossed the window open and leaned out. "Wilton! What are you doing with her on your horse?"

The overseer cast a brief glance in Trey's direction before he brought his riding crop down hard on the horse's flank, sending the animal into a fast trot.

Trey whirled away from the window and quickly pulled on his trousers. Running from his room and down the hall, he leapt down the stairs. Surprised to find it unbolted, Trey yanked open the side door. He rushed onto the side veranda. The stable was behind the house. He prayed that he could get his horse, Danton, saddled and on the road in time to rescue Carlee.

He could still hear her calling out to him. "Trey! Please help me, Trey!"

"I'm coming, Carlee. I'm coming!"

He jumped off the veranda and ran towards the stables, ignoring the pain as his bare feet encountered various bits of stones. The big doors were open. He rushed inside and collided with a tall, well-built man exiting the stables.

The collision with his father sent him sprawling onto his back. "Father!" He scrambled to his knees and grabbed his father's legs. "Wilton has Carlee! He's taking her away! You must stop him!"

His father didn't respond.

Bounding to his feet, Trey ran for his horse. He had his saddle in his hands when his father turned him around.

One look in his father's eyes and he knew why the side door had been unbolted in the middle of the night.

"He's taking her with your permission, Father?"

"Yes."

Trey swallowed a wave of rage at the terse word from his father. "Well not with mine!" He jerked away and tossed his saddle aside, deciding to ride bareback. Before he could mount his horse, his father grabbed him and pushed him against the side of the stall. He could no longer hear Carlee's cries. His heart thundered and fear tightened his throat. "Get out of my way, Father!"

"I sold her, Trey."

"Sold her? But you gave her to me! You can't sell her. She's mine!"

His father's hands tightened on his upper arms, holding him still. "That happened when you were seven and I never expected you to fall for her. In this family, we do not bed our slaves, boy!"

His heart sank. His mother had not kept her word. She had told his father about seeing him kissing Carlee the previous week. "I know that, Father, and I have not bedded her! I give you my word!"

"And I believe you, Trey. We Brandauers are not known for being liars."

He tried to pull away. "Then let me go and get her. She's mine. I will not have her sold away from me and her family."

"She is already sold. I believe that you haven't touched her, but I have seen the way you two look at each other. You are no longer children, Trey. I can't allow you to father children with her."

He sucked in a shuddering breath. At seventeen, he longed to discover sex with the fifteen-year-old Carlee. Still, he'd never gone beyond an occasional hug or a rare, brief peck at her sweet lips. He hadn't even dared touch her breasts. The temptation had been difficult to resist since he had inadvertently seen her sleek, nude body as she had bathed in the pond deep in the woods early one morning.

He had longed to strip and join her. The thought of seeing the hurt and confusion in her brown eyes if he betrayed her trust had been enough to cool his passions. He had forced himself to steal quietly away instead.

"Please, Father. I promise...I give you my word. I will not touch her! Just please don't sell her!"

"It wasn't an easy decision, Trey, but it was a necessary one. I've made sure she's going to a good home where she'll be treated properly." His father reached in his pocket and produced a large sack filled with bills. "This is yours...for her sale."

The wall of rage consumed him. He jerked away from his father, slapped the sack out of his hand, placed his hands against his father's chest, and pushed as hard as he could.

Taken by surprise, his father stumbled backwards and fell.

Trey turned and jumped onto Danton's back, wheeled him around, sent him jumping over his father's body, and galloping out into the night.

He rode Danton hard and fast, ignoring his father's outraged shouts for him to return. He knew he was in more trouble than he'd ever been before for having shoved his father. Nevertheless, he had to save Carlee. After what seemed like an eternity, he heard soft wails that he knew belonged to her.

"Carlee! I'm coming!" he called.

"Trey! Oh, Trey!" He heard the relief in her voice. "I knew you would save me, Trey."

He rode low over Danton's back, taking a curve in the road quickly. He spotted Wilton, at least thirty or forty yards in front of him.

He dug his heels into Danton's flanks and urged him on. Danton was a better horse than the one ridden by Wilton. Elation filled Trey. He wasn't sure what he was going to do after he rescued her, but he was only moments away from getting her back.

He would worry about the consequences later.

Danton steadily closed the distance between him and Wilton. Soon, he would be close enough to reach out and snatch Carlee off Wilton's horse. He heard the sound of a galloping horse behind him.

"Trey! Come back here now or there will be hell to pay!"

He cast a quick glance over his shoulder.

His father charged after him, astride the only stallion in the county capable of outrunning Danton.

He leaned low over Danton's back. "You can do it," he whispered to Danton. "You can outrun Lightning. Just this once, Danton. You can do it for Carlee. Run like the wind, Danton. You can do it."

Within a few horse lengths of Wilton, Lightning drew even with Danton. His father snatched him off Danton's back and onto Lightning's. Danton continued running as his father pulled on Lightning's reins, urging him to an abrupt stop.

Trey struggled to be free. "Let me go! Please!" Although he was strong, his father was bigger and far stronger. His father's arms tightened around him, immobilizing him.

Trey watched Wilton's horse disappear around a bend in the road. "No! Carlee! Carlee, I'll find you. I promise. I swear. No matter how long it takes, I'll find and rescue you! And when I do I will never leave you again!"

"Trey! I'll wait...I'll wait for you to come, Trey!"

His father wheeled Lightning around and sent him galloping back towards the house Trey would never think of as home again. He slumped back against his father, bitter tears streaming down his cheeks. "Let me go rescue her, Father, or I swear I will never forgive you."

"I know this hurts now, Trey, but this is for the best. I need you to understand why I had to do this."

"You didn't. I would have kept my word."

"I know you have good intentions, boy, but you would be sneaking into her bed eventually. Do you understand? "

"I won't ever forgive you for this, Father."

His father pulled up his horse and turned his face up to his. He saw something he'd never seen before — tears in his father's eyes. "I didn't do this easily, Trey. I know this hurts you and it hurts me, but I had to do it. I had to. You'll forgive me because it was done out of love."

He shook his head. "No. I won't ever forgive you for this. You don't know what you've done. I'll never be happy again if I don't find her. You have to tell me where she's going."

"I know it hurts boy, but in time you'll forget her and move on. You'll marry and have children and be happy."

"I'll never be happy without her. Never. And I will never forgive you for this."

"Time has a way of healing all wounds, Trey."

"Time will never heal this wound. Nor will I ever forgive you or Mother."

Marilyn Lee

Soul Mates is available from Marilyn Lee Unleashed

Marilyn's booklist:

Marilyn Lee Unleashed

Shana Mine
Dream Lover
A Cheating Situation
Any Time Any Place
Beauty Is Alisha Hoover?
Blue Desert Heat 1
Blue Desert Heat 2
Blue Desert Tales: Courtesan Seduction
Daughters of Takira: One Night In Vegas
Daughters of Takira 2: Kyla's Awakening
Daughters of Takira 3: Revelations
Falling Hard
Fantasy Knights
Fantasy Knights 2: Endless Love
In Blood 2-Lost Without
Large, Shy & Beautiful
Loving Large — Yours, Only And Always
Loving Large 2 — Yours, Now And Forever
Marilyn Lee Omnibus I
Marilyn Lee Sampler
Marilyn Lee Sampler 2
My Mother's Man
No Commitment Required: Naughty Girls
Primal Lusts
Secondhand Lover
Secret Lover
Some Like It Male
Soul Mates
Taking Chances: Falling For Sharde

Taking Chances 2: Nice Girls Do
The Dare
The Quest 1: Hunter's Passion
Torn By Love
Where You Find It
Yesterday's Secret Sins


Red Rose Publishing

Sweet Surrender
Sister's Keeper
Finding Love Again
Betrayed By Love
Song of Desire
It Had To Be You
One Sweet Night
Tempting Neal
In Blood And Worth Loving
Eye of the Beholder
Night Heat
A Thing Called Love
Summer Storm
Skin Deep


Ellora's Cave
Night of Sin
Bloodlust series:
Conquering Mikhel Dumont
The Talisman
The Taming Serge Dumont
Forbidden Desires
Nocturnal Heat

Midnight Shadows
All In The Family

Moonlight series:
Moonlight Desire
Moonlight Whispers

Long Line of Love series:
Night of Desires
Love Out Loud
Only One Love

Teacher's Pet
Trina's Afternoon Delight
Branded
Road To Rapture
The Fall of Troy
Full Bodied Charmer
Breathless In Black
Playing With Fire
White Christmas
Quest II — Divided Loyalties
Quest III — Return to Volter


Changeling Press

Moonlight Madness
Bloodlust — Nighttime Magic
Marilyn's homepage: http://www.marilynlee.org

Email: marilynlee@marilynlee.org

## Marilyn's Bio:

Marilyn Lee lives, works, and writes on the East Coast. In addition to thoroughly enjoying writing erotic romances, she enjoys roller-skating, spending time with her large, extended family, and rooting for all her hometown sports teams. Her other interests include collecting Doc Savage pulp novels from the thirties and forties and collecting Marvel comics from the seventies and eighties (particularly Thor and The Avengers). Her favorite TV shows are forensic shows, westerns (Gunsmoke and Have Gun, Will Travel are particular favorites), mysteries (loves the old Charlie Chan mysteries. Her all time favorite mystery movie is probably Dead, Again), and nearly every vampire movie or television show ever made (Forever Knight and Count Yorga, Vampire are favorites). Marilyn has won numerous writing accolades, including a CAPA award for Bloodlust: Conquering Mikhel Dumont and the following Lub-Dubs Awards for 2009: Lifetime Achievement Award, In Blood And Worth Loving (Best erotic novel and best sci-fi/fantasy/paranormal Award.
She loves to hear from readers who can email her at Mlee2057@AOL.com or who can visit her website, http://www.marilynlee.org. She has a Yahoo! Group called Love Bytes that readers can join by sending an email to: marilynlee-subscribe@yahoogroups.com

16087523R10071

Made in the USA
Lexington, KY
03 July 2012